# angel

## Belinda Ray

SCHOLASTIC INC.

New York  Toronto  London  Auckland  Sydney
Mexico City  New Delhi  Hong Kong  Buenos Aires

ISBN 0-439-56011-X

Copyright © 2003 17th Street Productions,
an Alloy company
All rights reserved.
Published by Scholastic Inc.

Produced by 17th Street Productions,
an Alloy company
151 West 26th Street
New York, NY 10001

12 11 10 9 8 7 6 5 4          4 5 6 7 8/0

Printed in the U.S.A.          40
First printing, October 2003

# CHAPTER
## One

"Okay, class," Mrs. Wessex said in her usual cheery voice. "Clear off your desks. It's time for our vocabulary test."

Several students moaned as they placed their books on the floor, but not Anna Lee. She didn't mind tests. Back at her old school, all of Anna's friends had envied her amazing memory. She could read something just once and have it memorized. It was a skill that made studying for tests—and acing them—pretty easy.

Everyone had considered her the smartest student in the class, but Anna had been pretty popular at her old school, too. She got invited to all of the birthday parties, received a ton of cards on Valentine's Day, and was even voted "Most Spirited" at last year's fourth-grade field day competition. But that was back at Jackson

Intermediate School. Elizabeth Cady Stanton Middle School was completely different.

Here no one seemed to have noticed how smart Anna was or how well she did on tests. Or if they had, they didn't care. As for birthday parties, she hadn't heard about any yet, and the only title she'd earned so far was "the-new-girl." Or, as Anna saw it, "the-new-girl-with-no-friends."

"All right," Mrs. Wessex said, adjusting her glasses. Anna had Mrs. Wessex for both English and social studies. "Is everybody ready?" She looked around the room and smiled pleasantly at Anna. Then she raised her gaze slightly. Matt Dana, the boy who sat directly behind Anna, had his hand in the air.

"Yes, Matthew?" Mrs. Wessex called.

"I need to sharpen my pencil," he replied.

A few girls giggled. Anna rolled her eyes. Matt Dana *always* needed to sharpen his pencil.

In the three days that Anna had been attending Elizabeth Cady Stanton Middle School, Matt Dana had asked for permission to sharpen his pencil approximately ninety-six times. Secretly, Anna believed that if she turned around quick and caught him by surprise, she'd see him chewing the tip off just so that he could get up and sharpen it again.

"Quickly," Mrs. Wessex told him. Matt sprang to his feet and headed for the pencil sharpener at the front of the room. "Walk, please," Mrs. Wessex warned him, and he slowed his sprint to a shuffling jog.

*Lead-eater,* Anna thought as he passed her desk.

"All right," Mrs. Wessex went on. "While Matthew is taking care of that, I need someone to help pass out the tests." Twenty arms shot into the air, but Mrs. Wessex ignored them all. "Anna—could you come up here, please?" she asked.

Anna swallowed hard. Why did teachers always do that? Call on the one person who hadn't raised her hand? Ugh. The only thing worse than being the-new-girl-with-no-friends was being the-new-girl-with-no-friends-standing-up-in-front-of-the-whole-class.

"Anna?" Mrs. Wessex repeated.

Reluctantly, Anna rose from her chair. On the other side of the room, Lauren Graham whispered something to Maria Mancini, and they both giggled. Anna's cheeks burned. Were they talking about her?

*Just ignore them,* she told herself. She wasn't going to let a few giggles intimidate her.

"Five per row," Mrs. Wessex said, handing Anna a stack of papers.

"Okay," Anna said with a nod. Then she turned and began counting out papers for the girl at the front of the first line of desks. Her name was Theresa Allen, and she wore her long brown hair in cornrows that spilled around her shoulders.

Anna thought about asking how long it had taken to make all those tiny braids and who had done it for her—and how they stayed in place when she washed her hair—but instead she just handed Theresa the tests. "Here."

"Thanks," Theresa said with a wide grin. Then she leaned forward slightly. "I like your shirt," she confided quietly.

"Me, too," Carrie Weingarten whispered from the next desk back. Carrie was Theresa's best friend. The two of them were practically inseparable.

More than once Anna had walked down the hall behind them, watching Carrie's bright red curls bouncing up and down as Theresa's thin brown braids swayed from side to side. They were always talking and giggling, and they seemed really nice.

"It's really cool," Theresa added. "Where did you get it?"

Anna's almond-shaped eyes widened. She

glanced down, having completely forgotten what shirt she was wearing. It was a simple white peasant blouse—nothing special, really—but her grandmother had embroidered tiny red flowers around the wide cuffs and square neckline.

Anna felt a smile creep onto her face. She was just about to say "thank you" when the girl at the head of the next row spoke up.

"*Hel-lo?* I'd like to take my test *this year*, if you don't mind," Sharon Ross said. All the kids around her giggled—especially Kimberly Price, who seemed to think that everything Sharon said was hilarious.

"Anna—please don't dawdle," Mrs. Wessex instructed her.

"Sorry," Anna said. She felt her cheeks go red again, and she was so flustered, she forgot all about thanking Theresa and Carrie. Instead, she lowered her eyes and started toward Sharon's desk, counting out another five tests.

Unfortunately, in that same instant, Matt Dana finished sharpening his pencil and turned to sprint back to his seat. In less than two strides, he crashed into Anna, sending her and all the test papers—except for the five she'd already handed out—flying.

"Hey!" Anna yelled, trying to regain her balance. But before she knew what had happened, she found herself lying on her stomach on the red-and-white-tiled floor, with Matt Dana sprawled across her legs and papers fluttering down all around her. Everyone in the room howled.

"All right, settle down, everyone," Mrs. Wessex said. The laughter began to subside as Mrs. Wessex knelt next to Anna. "Are you okay?" she asked.

"I guess," Anna said, scowling at Matt.

"I didn't mean to," he protested.

"Wow, that's the first time I've seen someone fall down handing out tests," Sharon said, causing another surge of giggles in the classroom.

Anna narrowed her eyes. "I didn't *fall.* He—"

"All right, all right," Mrs. Wessex interrupted. Anna glared at Sharon. She'd made it sound like Anna was a klutz, when really Matt was to blame. Why wasn't anyone laughing at *him*?

Anna tried to stare Sharon down, but Sharon's gaze was unflinching, and Mrs. Wessex shifted, blocking Anna's view.

"How about you, Matthew?" Mrs. Wessex asked. "Are you hurt?"

"No," he said. "I'm fine."

"Okay, then," Mrs. Wessex said, offering each of them a hand. "Why don't the two of you return to your seats? I'll take care of the tests."

Anna stood up slowly, aware of a tender spot on her right knee. She was sure to have a first-rate black-and-blue there by the end of the day. Limping, she returned to her desk. No sooner had she sat down than she felt a tap on her shoulder.

"Hey, I'm sorry," Matt Dana whispered. Anna sighed. He sounded sincere, but she couldn't help it—she was still upset. He could apologize all day long and it wouldn't make a difference.

Thanks to him, she was no longer the-new-girl-with-no-friends. She wasn't even the-new-girl-with-no-friends-standing-up-in-front-of-the-whole-class. Now she was the-new-girl-with-no-friends-who-had-fallen-flat-on-her-face. It wasn't exactly a step in the right direction.

# CHAPTER
## Two

During recess and lunch, Anna laid low. It was pretty easy to do. No one missed her in the kickball game, no one missed her in the circles of friends laughing and talking, and no one missed her at any of the tables in the cafeteria.

In fact, aside from one of the lunch ladies, no one even spoke to her until she was on her way back to class.

"Hey, Anna!" Sharon Ross called out as Anna was opening her locker. "Did you have a nice *trip*?"

"Good one," Kimberly Price hooted, slapping her friend's hand. Anna closed her eyes and tried to ignore their laughter, but it was no use. She was tired. Tired of being new, tired of being alone, and tired of being laughed at.

It had only been ten days since she'd left

Doncaster, California, but it felt like years had passed. The sunny beaches with their warm sand and big blue waves seemed worlds away from New Hampshire, this land of gray skies and cold spring rain. And the fact that she hadn't managed to make any friends yet didn't help.

At Anna's old school, she'd had plenty of friends. Fifteen kids had come to her going-away party! If only she could be back there now. But she was stuck here, in Newcastle, New Hampshire. Alone. And so sick of it, she felt like crying.

"Anna?"

Anna felt her shoulders tighten. She pressed her eyes closed and fought back the tears, bracing herself for the next joke. Sharon could tease her all she wanted, but Anna wasn't going to cry. She wouldn't give Sharon—or Kimberly—the satisfaction.

"*Anna*," the voice repeated. "Come on. You're going to be late for class."

Slowly, Anna looked up, surprised to see Carrie Weingarten standing beside her. *Smiling*.

"Oh . . . um . . ." Anna glanced around. She and Carrie were the only ones in the hallway.

"Let's go," Carrie said, tugging Anna's elbow.

"Uh . . . okay," Anna stammered. She grabbed her math book and followed Carrie's bouncing mass of curly red hair down the hall to Mr. Kane's room.

"I hate being late for math," Carrie confided as they walked. "Whenever I am, Mr. Kane always says something embarrassing like, 'I'm glad you could find the time to join us, Carrie,' and then everyone stares at me and I feel so stupid."

Anna snorted. "Try falling on your face in front of the whole class."

"Ooh—that's right," Carrie said with a wince. "I almost forgot. But that wasn't your fault. And besides—you handled it really well."

"I *did*?"

"Yeah," Carrie said with a shrug. "You just got up and went back to your seat like it was no big deal. I would've died of embarrassment."

*Wow*, Anna thought. Carrie didn't seem to think she was a total loser—she actually thought Anna had handled the situation well. And she realized it hadn't been Anna's fault.

Anna wished she had more time to talk to Carrie. It seemed like they reached Mr. Kane's room way too soon.

"Thanks for joining us, ladies," he bellowed

as they entered. Carrie shot Anna a sideways glance, and Anna smirked. Sometimes teachers were *so* predictable. "Go ahead and take a seat."

Anna hurried toward the back of the room, following Carrie's lead. When Theresa saw Carrie approaching, she moved a red jacket from the chair next to hers. Thankfully, there was another free seat at the table for Anna. It was next to Matt Dana, but Anna tried not to let that bother her. After all, he hadn't *meant* to make her look like an idiot in front of everyone. And at least now she knew that not *everyone* thought she was.

"Hey, Anna," Theresa said as Anna sat down. "Where were you at recess? I wanted to ask you about your shirt. You never told me where you got it."

"Oh, right," Anna said. "We sort of got interrupted." She stole a look at Sharon Ross, surprised to see that Sharon was staring right back at her. What was her problem, anyway? Anna turned back to Theresa. "I got it at this shop in Venice Beach, but my grandmother did the embroidery."

"Cool," Theresa said. "I really like it."

"You lived near Venice Beach?" Matt Dana asked, looking up from whatever he was working on in his notebook.

"Sort of," Anna started. "I mean—"

"Okay, people, listen up," Mr. Kane called out. He was moving about the room, handing work sheets to each table. "Today we're going to have a little contest," he said. "I've given each table the same set of work sheets, and we're going to see which group can work together to finish theirs the fastest."

Anna glanced at the others and raised her eyebrows. It sounded like fun.

"The winners," Mr. Kane continued, eyeing each table in turn, "will get a special prize at the end of class."

Theresa grinned. "I like prizes," she whispered, and for a moment, Anna forgot all about being the new girl. She loved games and contests of all sorts, and math was her favorite subject. She smiled back at Theresa and Carrie. She even smiled at Matt Dana.

The class was silent as everyone watched Mr. Kane for their cue to start. As the second hand on the clock approached twelve, he put his hand in the air. "Okay . . . go!" he said, lowering his arm like he was starting a race. Anna reached out a hand, but not fast enough. Theresa quickly grabbed all the work sheets.

Back at Jackson Intermediate, Anna would

have been the one to take charge, and all of her friends would have expected her to—but not here. Here no one thought of her as a leader. In fact, no one really knew anything about her, which meant she was going to have to prove herself all over again.

Anna sighed. She was already sick of this starting-over business, and she hadn't even been at it that long. Still, she wished she could just skip ahead. Or fast-forward to the good part. *The part where I fit in and feel comfortable and have plenty of friends and things to do and parties to go to and—*

"All right, let's see what we've got," Theresa mumbled, flipping through the papers. "Metric measuring. There are sixteen things to measure in the classroom—we should split those up and each do four," she said, setting that work sheet aside. "Then there's graphing—"

"I'll take that one," Matt Dana said, and before Theresa could reply, he snatched it out of her hands and went straight to work on it.

"O-*kay*," Theresa said, glancing at Carrie and Anna with a shrug. "So that leaves two work sheets—one on figuring out the areas and perimeters of a bunch of shapes and one on . . . *oh, no.*" She grimaced as she looked at the last paper.

"What is it?" Carrie asked.

"Adding, subtracting, and multiplying fractions," Theresa said with a groan. "I hate fractions."

"I'll do it," Anna offered. She'd always found fractions easy.

"Are you sure?" Theresa asked.

"Yep," Anna said with a nod, and, following Matt Dana's lead, she snatched it from Theresa's hand and set to work.

"Okay," Carrie said, "but don't worry if you don't finish them all. Theresa and I will split up these other problems, and when we're done, we'll help you with the fractions."

"Or Matt can help when he's done with the graphing," Theresa suggested. "Right, Matt?"

"Sure," Matt said without looking up. He had already plotted out half of the points on his graph paper, and it looked like his final picture was going to be some kind of bird.

"Okay, Anna?" Carrie asked.

Anna nodded again, but she was barely paying attention. She'd already finished the first two problems on her sheet, and she was determined to get the rest done on her own, too.

After about fifteen minutes, Matt Dana set down his pencil and looked up. "Great horned owl," he said, showing the picture to the rest of the group.

"Awesome," Theresa said. "Now can you help Anna finish the fractions?" But before he could answer, Anna set down her pencil as well.

"Done," she said.

"*What?*" Carrie asked, her hazel eyes as wide as nickels.

Theresa squinted. "You're kidding," she said.

Anna couldn't help smiling. "Nope. They're all finished." The rest of her group stared at her silently. "They were easy ones," she added modestly.

"Easy *fractions?*" Theresa said. "Is there such a thing?" Anna shrugged. She didn't know what to say. If she made it sound like they had been too easy for her, the others might think she was conceited. Thankfully, Matt broke the silence.

"Come on. Let's get measuring so we can win this thing," he said. "I'll take the first four problems, and you can start on five through eight."

"Okay," Anna said. She took out her ruler and set off to measure the tissue box, an electrical outlet, and the length and width in centimeters of her desk and her social studies book. By the time she had completed her first measurement, Theresa and Carrie had finished their work sheet and began their measuring, too.

They finished quickly, and with ten minutes left in class, Theresa arranged all four work sheets in a neat stack and ran up to give them to Mr. Kane. She beat Sharon Ross by just five seconds.

"So did we do it?" Carrie asked when Theresa returned to her seat. "Did we win?"

"I don't know," Theresa said. "Mr. Kane said that since our group and Sharon's group finished so close together, he was going to check all the answers and see who got the most right."

Anna glanced over at Sharon's table and gulped. Sharon's brown eyes were trained on her with the intensity of a cat stalking its prey. What was *with* that girl?

As other students handed in their work sheets, the classroom began to buzz with excitement. Everyone wanted to know which group had won, and Mr. Kane had made it clear that even the late finishers had a chance if the first groups done had made too many errors.

Finally, with only three minutes to go before the end of class, Mr. Kane stood up from his desk. "Okay!" he said. "We're down to two groups." A hush fell over the classroom. "We've got Sharon, Kimberly, Jeremy, and Billy . . . and Theresa, Carrie, Matt, and Anna."

Carrie reached out and grabbed Theresa's hand. Then she reached across the table and grabbed Anna's, too, squeezing it hard. Anna squeezed back. She wanted to win—partly because it would be fun to be part of a winning team, but mostly because it would feel so good to beat Sharon after all of her rude comments and mean stares.

"Both groups have gotten every answer correct so far, and all I've got left to look at are the fractions," Mr. Kane told them. "So . . . Lauren, why don't you take the work sheet from Sharon's group, and Maria, you take the one from Theresa's group, and I'll read the answers out loud. Ready?"

Maria and Lauren sat up straight, each of them aware of the responsibility they'd been given. "Ready," they said at the same time.

As Mr. Kane called out the answers, they made large *C*s for "correct" next to each problem. Anna leaned forward and watched Maria closely, sighing with each *C* but dreading that the next mark she made would be an *X*.

"I know ours are right," Sharon told her group. "I did them all myself."

Theresa, Carrie, and Matt shot nervous glances at Anna, and Anna bit her lip. She was pretty sure her answers were right, too, but she wasn't about to say so. It sounded pretty arrogant. Plus, there was always the possibility that she had missed one, especially since she had been trying to finish them so fast.

But when Mr. Kane had read the last answer, Anna could see that her paper was covered with nothing but *C*s.

"What's the total, ladies?" Mr. Kane asked.

"These are all right," Maria said. Matt Dana offered his hand to Anna for a high five, and she slapped it.

"How about yours, Lauren?" Mr. Kane asked.

"One wrong," Lauren said.

Carrie and Theresa squealed.

"Let me see that!" Sharon demanded.

"One-half plus one-third is five-sixths," Lauren told her, pointing at the problem in question.

*"One-third?"* Sharon said. "I thought it said *one-eighth*. Mr. Kane, that's not fair," she protested. "I didn't get it wrong—I misread it."

"Well, next time you'll just have to be more careful," Mr. Kane told her. "But right now, I'd like to present our winners with their prizes." He walked over to Anna's table and gave her, Theresa, Carrie, and Matt each a certificate good for a free ice cream or milk shake at Ed's Soda Shoppe, a local ice cream place.

"Cool," Matt said.

"Awesome work, everybody," Carrie told the group. "Especially you, Anna," she added.

"Yeah," Theresa agreed, grinning across the table. "Will you be in our group next time we have a contest?"

"Sure," Anna replied. Did they actually think there was a chance she would say no? Maybe they hadn't noticed that she had no friends. Then again, maybe that was about to change.

Theresa and Carrie seemed really nice, and they *had* invited Anna to work with them again. Maybe today was the day Anna was finally going to make some friends at her new school.

# CHAPTER
# Three

Or maybe not.

Anna was putting on her jacket when she heard familiar voices nearby.

"Do you know what's better than black raspberry chocolate chip ice cream in a sugar cone?" she heard Carrie say.

"No—what?" Theresa's voice replied.

"*Free* black raspberry chocolate chip ice cream in a sugar cone," Carrie replied, and the two of them giggled. They were just a few lockers down, but there were enough people in between that Anna could sneak glances without being noticed.

"I'm so psyched we won the math contest," Theresa said.

"I know," Carrie answered. "That was awesome. But did you see Sharon's face when Lauren said she got one wrong?"

"Oh, my gosh," Theresa said. "She was so red, I thought she was going to burst into flames."

"Or tear Lauren's arm off getting her paper back," Carrie added. "You know, I think that's the first time Sharon's lost one of those contests in over a month."

*Wow*, Anna thought. *No wonder she was giving me death glares all through social studies.* Then again, getting death glares from Sharon wasn't anything new. Anna had been receiving them since her very first day at ECS.

The first one had come right after she'd spelled *tintinnabulation* correctly to win a mock spelling bee in English class. Sharon had left out an *n* on her turn.

The second death glare had been given later that same day, when Anna had been the only one to solve a logic problem Mr. Kane had written on the chalkboard. Since then, they'd been coming steadily—three yesterday, four today, and if the pattern held, she had five to look forward to tomorrow.

So death glares were old news for Anna. But speaking to Carrie and Theresa was something new. And thanks to the math contest, Anna had an easy opening so she could talk to them again soon.

All she needed to do was to walk over and ask them where Ed's Soda Shoppe was. It was a totally legitimate question—she had a free ice cream certificate to use. And once they told her where it was, it would be easy enough for Anna to ask if they wanted to go with her to get their ice cream.

It was a perfect plan, and Anna was ready to put it into action. She just needed to finish packing up her books. She was shoving her social studies homework into her notebook when she heard Carrie speak up.

"Hey, Resa—do you want to go to Ed's *today*?"

Anna peeked around the side of her locker door and watched nervously. If they decided to go today, that might make things even easier.

Theresa shrugged. "I don't know. Are you in the mood for ice cream?"

"Are you kidding? I'm *always* in the mood for ice cream," Carrie said.

"Oh, yeah, I forgot," Theresa said with a laugh. "Sure, why not?" She slammed her locker shut, hefted her backpack onto her shoulder, and stood waiting for Carrie.

Anna took a deep breath. In another minute, they'd be coming her way and she could ask them about Ed's and see if she could tag along.

"Hey," Carrie said as she closed her locker, "maybe we should see if Matt and Anna want to come. I mean, we did win the certificates as a team—maybe we should celebrate together."

Anna's heart jumped into her throat. She had to be hearing things.

"Yeah—that would be cool," Theresa agreed. "Let's ask them."

*Ask them?* Anna thought. Maybe her luck was finally changing.

"Hey, Theresa! Carrie! Hold up!" Sharon Ross called. Anna's heart fell. It was uncanny how Sharon could be heard so easily above everyone else.

Anna glanced over to see her racing down the hall.

"Hurry up, Kimberly!" Sharon shouted over her shoulder. "We're going to miss the bus." Kimberly Price shuffled along behind Sharon, carrying a backpack that was almost as big as she was.

*Oh, yeah, my luck's changing,* Anna thought. *For the worse.*

"Okay, let's go," Sharon said as soon as she and Kimberly had reached Theresa and Carrie.

"Sharon got *Make It Real* on DVD," Kimberly

gushed, "and we're going to watch the second ending."

"That sounds cool, but . . ." Carrie's voice trailed off, and she shot a nervous look at Theresa.

"We're going to Ed's," Theresa finished for her.

"*Ed's?*" Sharon asked with a bit of a sneer. Carrie stared at the floor, but Theresa held Sharon's gaze.

"Yeah—have you seen Matt or Anna?" she asked. "We were going to invite them along— you know, since they were on our team."

"How could I forget?" Sharon grumbled. "But you *can't* be serious."

"Why not?" Theresa asked.

"Are you kidding?" Sharon said. "Anna Lee is a total loser. She's so quiet. And boring. And did you see the way she fell all over herself in English class? She's such a klutz, she'd probably spill her ice cream on you."

*Klutz?!* Anna was two seconds away from slamming her locker and storming over there when Carrie spoke up.

"*Sharon,*" she said.

Anna froze. It sounded like Carrie was going to defend her. If she did, Anna would know for certain that she had made her first friend.

*Come on, Carrie,* she wished. *Tell her to quit it.*

"What?" Sharon snapped. "Didn't you see her?"

Anna peeked around her locker door just in time to see Carrie shrug and stare at the floor again. Thankfully, Theresa came to her rescue.

"Come on, Sharon—it wasn't that bad," she said. "It wasn't even Anna's fault. It was Matt's."

*Yeah,* thought Anna. *You go, Theresa.*

"It was *not*," Sharon argued. "She stepped right in front of him. 'How many papers, Ms. Wessex?'" she mimicked in a meek, high-pitched voice. "'Five? I'm not sure I can count that high—aahhhhhooooooops!'"

Anna didn't have to look to know that Sharon was imitating her.

"That was perfect!" Kimberly squealed.

Anna waited for Theresa to speak up—to tell them that it wasn't perfect and that it wasn't funny, either. She waited . . . and waited . . . and waited. Nothing. Finally, she sneaked a glance in their direction, and what she saw made her jaw drop. Theresa was smiling, and so was Carrie. And even though they weren't exactly laughing, they did look amused.

"Why was she sitting with you in math class, anyway?" Sharon asked.

Anna was beginning to wonder the same thing. If they really liked her, they'd tell Sharon to stop making fun of her—wouldn't they?

"I guess because we walked to class together," Carrie said. She was speaking so quietly that Anna had to strain to hear her.

"Well, I guess you won't make that mistake twice," Sharon joked as Kimberly chortled. Their voices were plenty loud.

Anna was stunned. How could someone be so mean? Sharon barely even knew Anna. Why did she hate her so much? *And why weren't Carrie and Theresa saying anything?*

"Actually," Theresa started, her voice almost as quiet as Carrie's now, "we invited her to be on our team next time, too."

Anna sucked in her breath. There was still hope. There was still a chance that Theresa and Carrie wanted to be her friends.

"You *invited* her?" Sharon repeated. *"Why?"*

*Because they like me,* Anna thought. *Go on, tell her.*

But it was silent. And the longer the silence dragged on, the worse Anna felt. How hard was it to explain that they wanted her on their team? Or that they didn't think she was so bad? Or that maybe—just maybe—she was even kind of cool?

"I don't know," Theresa finally answered. "I guess because she's smart."

"You think she's *smart*?" Sharon sneered.

"Yeah," Carrie said. "I mean, she always gets the right answers when Mr. Kane calls on her in class. Even for the hard stuff."

*That was it?* Anna's shoulders slumped forward. She felt like she'd been punched in the stomach. Two minutes ago, she'd believed she was on the verge of making friends, but now she knew the truth. They'd only wanted her to help them win the contest.

"Whatever," Sharon said. "She's still a loser. And anyway—we have to go if we're going to make the bus."

"But what about Ed's?" Theresa asked.

"We can go there after the video," Sharon said. "If we see Matt on the way to the bus, you can invite him. He's cool. But forget about Anna. There won't be any math contests at Ed's." Theresa and Carrie—and of course, Kimberly—giggled.

"All right. Let's go," Theresa said.

As the four girls moved toward her, Anna tried to make herself invisible. She practically dove into her locker. If she could have fit inside, she would have closed the door and stayed there.

And why not? It wasn't as if anyone would have missed her.

Anna walked home in the mist, wishing she had brought the umbrella her mother had tried to give her that morning. When were these gray days going to end, anyway? It had been cold and rainy ever since Anna and her family had arrived. Back in California, all the flowers were already in bloom, but spring still seemed to be at least a month away here in New Hampshire.

By the time Anna reached her house, her short black hair hung heavily at the sides of her head, dripping onto her neck and shoulders. She swung open the wooden front door and stepped inside, hanging her jacket on its wall peg and removing her shoes.

"How was school, honey?" her mother called from the kitchen.

Anna answered the same way she had the last two days. "Fine."

"Did you learn anything new?"

*Let's see . . . I'm lame and a total loser,* thought Anna, but she knew that answer wouldn't go over well with her mother. Mrs. Lee would either lecture Anna on the importance of maintaining a positive attitude or, worse, get out her

*Talking to Your Preteen* book and start asking Anna questions like, "Are you starting to feel confused about boys, honey?"

*No, thank you,* Anna thought. It was easier to just answer her mother's questions and get them over with.

"Ummm," Anna murmured as she walked into the kitchen. She had to come up with something. Her mother wouldn't accept no for an answer. Every day she insisted that Anna and her older brother, Kim, come up with at least one new thing they'd learned that day.

"I know," Anna said finally. "One-half plus one-third is five-sixths."

"Very good," her mother replied. "But didn't you know that before?"

"Not really. I mean, I could have figured it out before," Anna said, "but now I have it memorized. That's new."

Her mother stopped chopping vegetables and squinted at her. "I guess it is," she agreed after a moment. Then she picked up a potato and started to peel it. Slivers of potato flew into the sink as she worked.

"Where's Kim?" Anna asked.

"He went to play baseball with some friends," Mrs. Lee answered without looking up. *Friends?* Anna thought. Kim had already made friends? And enough for a baseball team?

"What about Gran?" Anna asked.

"Volunteering at the soup kitchen with that seniors group she joined," Mrs. Lee replied.

Anna shook her head. Even her *grandmother* had new people to hang out with. Apparently, Anna was the only loser in the family. She sat and watched her mother peel another potato. *Another exciting afternoon,* she thought. *Boy, is Kim going to be sorry he missed this.*

Finally, her mother set down the last of the freshly skinned potatoes and turned to her. "Are you okay, Anna?" *Uh-oh.* She had that concerned, furrowed-eyebrow look going. "Would you like something to snack on? Some apple? Carrot sticks?"

"No, thanks," Anna said. "I'm not really hungry. I think I'm just going to get started on my homework." She snatched a round carrot slice and a few cherry tomatoes from the salad her mother had made and ducked out before the strange questions about boys and body changes could start flying.

*Phew,* Anna thought, starting up the stairs. *That was a close one.* She ran her hand along the handrail as she climbed. It was just a thin bar attached to the wall, and its white paint was peeling.

In her old house, there had been a solid oak banister that ran the full length of the stairs, curving outward at the bottom. Anna used to love to slide down it. So did Kim, up until about a year ago. Now that he was fifteen, though, he considered himself too old for that kind of stuff. Not that it mattered. The banister was back in California, along with everything else Anna liked.

She plodded to her room, which was down at the end of the hall. The pale blue carpet that covered most of the upstairs was kind of cushy on her feet, but Anna preferred the hardwood floors of her old house.

As she passed Kim's room, she noticed that he'd found time to hang his DANGER ZONE: NO ENTRY sign on his closed door. Last night, she'd heard him tacking up posters and stuff, too. He didn't seem to be having any trouble settling in. And by now, he probably had a decent amount of dirty laundry on the floor, which meant that his room here was probably starting to look pretty much like his old room in California. Anna's, however, was still plain.

Its white walls depressed her. It seemed so

sterile, so devoid of personality. She hadn't taken the time to put up any of her old posters or unpack any of her books yet, so it didn't even feel like *her* room. It could have been anyone's, and right now it just felt like one more place where she didn't belong.

"How pathetic is that?" Anna muttered as she dropped her backpack on the floor. "Even *at home* I don't feel at home."

If only she could have stayed in Doncaster—at least to finish out the school year. Having to move away from all her friends was bad enough, but having to move in the middle of the year was even worse.

She'd begged her parents to let her stay with one of her friends—just until summer—but they wouldn't even consider it. They told her the family was staying together and that was that. End of discussion.

Kim had been kind of upset about the move, too, but it didn't seem to be bothering him anymore. He'd been lucky. The boy next door, Dylan McPhetres, was his age, and they'd hit it off right away. And now it sounded like Kim had made even more friends. He seemed to be doing really well with all of the recent changes. A lot better than Anna was, anyway.

She couldn't stop thinking about the fact that in just ten days, she'd gone from being kind of popular to being completely friendless. She'd been forced to leave the house she'd grown up in and move into one where she felt like a guest. She'd left behind a town where she knew every single shortcut and where to get the best pizza, to come to this place, where she couldn't even find the local ice cream parlor.

And she'd gone from an intermediate school, where the fifth graders ruled, to a middle school, where she was at the bottom of the ladder all over again. But the hardest part was having no friends. No one to talk to all day and no one to hang out with after school.

*Friends.* Like Caitlin and Leah.

Anna walked over to her bureau and opened a medium-sized box that was sitting on top of it. She took out an old diary, a few animal posters that were folded up, and finally, a small wooden jewelry box.

Inside, the box was lined with red velvet and separated into several compartments, but Anna's favorite part was the secret storage area. The top shelf lifted out to reveal a sunken area where Anna kept her most valuable jewelry—like the necklace Caitlin and Leah had given her as a going-away present.

When the three girls had been younger—they'd known each other since they were six—they'd really liked angels. They'd had angel posters on their walls, angel stickers on their notebooks, and matching angel T-shirts. They seemed to have outgrown their angel phase sometime around third grade, but when Anna was getting ready to move, Caitlin and Leah had pooled their money to buy her an angel necklace.

Anna held the gleaming silver chain in her hand and ran her thumb over the cool metal links. Then, flopping down on her bed, she spread the necklace out in front of her and examined the five tiny angel charms that dangled from it.

*Guardian angels,* Anna thought. She knew Caitlin and Leah had given her the necklace as sort of a good-luck charm. Unfortunately, it didn't seem to be working—not that good luck could really improve her situation, anyway. What Anna needed was to fit in at this new school. But after hearing Sharon, Kimberly, Theresa, and Carrie making fun of her, it didn't seem like she ever would.

*And why not?*

Anna scowled at the necklace. "Because I'm a loser," she said, poking the first angel with her index finger. "And a klutz," she added, prodding the second one. "And I'm boring and way too quiet," she continued, jabbing the third angel and then the fourth. "And that's why I'm never going to have any friends." On the word *friends,* Anna gave the fifth angel the hardest poke of all.

"Hey—watch it!" a strange voice suddenly exclaimed. Anna's mouth dropped open as the tiny form rolled backward slightly, then shot up into a standing position. And as it did, the charm changed from shining silver to full color, as if a wave of water had splashed over it and washed off its metallic finish. Plus, the angel had nearly doubled in size; she now stood a full inch and a half tall!

"Sheesh," the angel cried in a little voice. "What an attitude! I can see I've got a lot of work to do here."

Anna gaped as the small figure shook her head rapidly, like a wet dog after a bath. A tiny shining halo wiggled back and forth, finally settling in a crooked position. "Whew!" the angel exclaimed. "Crossing over always makes me so dizzy. They say you get used to it, but I don't know. Hey—you got anything to eat?"

# CHAPTER
# Four

"Oh, no," Anna whispered. "I've lost it. *All this time alone has made me crazy.*"

The angel cocked her head, tipping her crooked halo to the other side. "Crazy, shmazy," she said, dusting off her white blouse and pleated plaid skirt. "If you're crazy, I'm Jiminy Cricket, and last I checked, my legs weren't long and green."

Anna blinked rapidly. The little . . . *angel*—or whatever she was—had come completely free of the necklace, and now she was standing on Anna's bed, wearing what seemed to be a private-school uniform. She even had white knee-highs, although they were mostly hidden by her bulky black combat boots.

*Combat boots?* Anna narrowed her eyes. "What kind of dream is this?" she muttered.

"Angels don't wear combat boots and . . . skull-caps," she added, noticing the dark blue knit hat that covered most of the angel's straight red hair and rested just above her eyebrows.

"Says who?" replied the angel. Anna jumped. If this vision was a figment of her imagination, why did it keep talking back to her?

"Uhhh," Anna moaned. It was all she could manage with her mouth still hanging open. She touched her hand to her forehead, but it didn't feel hot. "Maybe I didn't eat enough at lunch today," she wondered aloud. "Or maybe—"

The angel clicked her tongue. *"Hel-lo?"* she said. "I'm still in the room. And I'm *re-al.*"

"You can't be," Anna replied, shaking her head. "It's not possible."

"Yeah, whatever. Possible, impossible, here I am. Go ahead, pinch yourself. Heck, pinch *me.*"

Anna reached out and grasped the angel's tiny arm between her thumb and forefinger.

"Ouch! Not so hard, Gargantua! You're, like, a hundred times bigger than I am. Have a little sensitivity!"

"You told me to pinch you," Anna said.

"Yeah—*pinch* me. Not squeeze the life out of me!"

Anna blinked. *"Sor-ry."*

The angel waved one hand. "Aw, forget about it," she said. "Hey—where's my . . . ?" Suddenly, she started turning in circles, looking all around the bed.

"What?" Anna asked, but the angel didn't answer. She just shook her head and walked over to the necklace.

"Ack. I hate it when this happens."

Anna watched as the angel reached down and grabbed a small silver stick with a ball at the end that was attached to the necklace. She planted her feet on the chain on either side of it and pulled with all her might.

"Urgh," the angel grunted as she tugged upward.

At first, it looked like she was fighting a losing battle, but on her fourth try, the stick came loose and the angel toppled over backward, landing in a heap.

"Are you okay?" Anna asked.

"Oof. I think so. This down comforter makes for a pretty soft landing—way better than the pepperoni pizza I landed on the last time I left my wand behind."

"Ewww," Anna sympathized.

"Yeah, it wasn't pretty. But I'm not here to talk to you about pizza. I'm here to talk to you about . . . oh, man." The angel wrinkled her nose.

"What?" Anna frowned.

"Oh, nothing," the angel replied. "It's just that . . . well . . . I'm here to talk to you about friends, which technically makes me the . . . oh, I can't even say it."

Anna slid off her bed and knelt on the floor so that she was eye to eye with the angel. "Say *what*?"

The little sprite shook her head and rolled her eyes. "All right, here goes: I'm here to talk to you about friends, which technically makes me . . . *the friendship angel*." She practically groaned the last three words.

"The *friendship angel*?" Anna repeated. "Are you kidding me? That's got to be, like, the corniest thing I've ever heard. What do you do? Fly around sprinkling magic dust on people to make them play nice?"

"Magic dust is for amateurs!" the angel snapped.

"Whoa—sorry," Anna said. "I didn't realize friendship angels were so *sensitive*," she added with a giggle.

"All right, all right," the angel replied. She put her hands on her hips and tapped her foot. "Are you just about done?"

"Yeah, I guess," Anna said. "I mean, I wouldn't want to upset you or anything. You might wave your wand and make me friendly." She giggled again, but the angel just scowled at her.

"Uh-huh," she said, still tapping her foot. "Good one. Got any more?"

"Ummm," Anna murmured, pretending to think it over. "I guess not. That's it."

"Good. Then let's get down to business."

"We've got business?" Anna asked. "What kind of business, friendship angel?"

"Would you stop calling me that?!" the angel demanded, stamping her foot.

Anna laughed. This little person might not be real—although Anna was becoming more and more convinced that she was, with every passing minute—but still, Anna had to admit . . . she was pretty entertaining.

"All right," Anna said. "What should I call you? I mean, do you have a name? Other than . . . well, you know."

"Oh, right. Sorry. I guess I never really introduced myself, did I? I'm Zadie."

"Zadie. Wow—that's a cool name."

"Yeah, I guess," Zadie replied. "Until you tack 'the friendship angel' onto the end of it."

Anna laughed again. "Well, don't worry. I

won't. But, um . . . what's all this friendship stuff about, anyway? Is that your job or something? To go around making friends with people?"

Zadie exhaled heavily. "*No-o.* Actually, this is my first friendship assignment. The last time I was in your world, I was on dream patrol—you know, planting ideas in people's heads while they sleep. And before that I had to help this woman finish a book she was writing. Boy— that was a tough assignment. Writers are such procrastinators."

"Jeez," Anna said. "That sounds kind of cool—especially the dream stuff. I'd like to plant a few ideas in my mother's head while she's asleep. Maybe I could get her to give me a bigger allowance—or buy me a CD player for my room. Then I could convince my brother to let me use his MP3 player, and I could burn a bunch of—"

"Earth to Anna!" the angel called, cupping her hands around her mouth.

"Huh? Oh," Anna said, turning back to the angel. "I guess I was getting a little carried away. But wait—I still don't get it. Why are you here?"

"*Hel-lo?*" Zadie said. "Figure it out. I'm the friendship angel, right?"

"Yeah."

"And I popped off *your* necklace, right?"

"Uh-huh," Anna agreed.

Zadie cocked her head. "Okay. Will everyone in the room who has *no* friends please raise her hand," she said, pretending to address a crowd of people.

"Hey!" Anna protested, catching on. "I have friends!"

*"In this state?"* Zadie asked.

"Well . . . *no*," Anna admitted. "But what are *you* supposed to do about that? Bonk people on the head and make them think I'm cool?"

"You *are* cool," Zadie said.

"Yeah, right. That's why I sit in my room playing with my jewelry every afternoon— because I'm so cool, I can't decide who to hang out with."

Zadie shook her head. "There's that attitude again. If you want to make friends, you're going to have to lose that."

"You mean I should *turn my frown upside down?*" Anna scoffed.

"Ewww, no way," Zadie said, wincing. "Because then that little dimple above your lips would be on your chin, and that would just look freaky."

In spite of herself, Anna had to laugh. "Yeah,

I guess it would," she agreed. "But then what am I supposed to—"

A knock on the door stopped Anna midsentence.

"Anna?" her mother's voice called. "Are you all right? Who are you talking to in there?"

# CHAPTER
# Five

"Quick—hide!" Anna said.

With one swift jump, Zadie launched herself onto Anna's head. She ran a few circles, trying to figure out which way to go, and finally slid down a strand of hair in the back. "Ouch!" Anna cried.

"What did you say?" her mother asked through the door.

"Nothing," Anna said. "I mean . . . come in."

Her mother stepped into the room and glanced around. "Were you talking to someone?" Mrs. Lee asked.

"No. Why? Who would I be talking to?" Anna blurted.

Her mother squinted at her. "Are you feeling all right?"

"Yeah. Fine. Perfect. Why?" Anna said. She

knew she was talking way too fast, but she couldn't seem to slow herself down.

"Anna," Mrs. Lee said. "What's going on? I know I heard voices in here."

"*Ohhh, voices,*" Anna repeated, stalling for time. "Right. That was just me. I was . . . practicing a poem I have to read out loud. For English. Tomorrow." That seemed to settle her mother down a little. Her gaze had changed from seriously worried to only half suspicious.

"That sounds interesting," Mrs. Lee said. "What poem?"

"Huh?"

"What's the *name* of the poem you're working on?"

"Oh, it's—" At that moment, Zadie must have lost her balance because Anna felt two quick footsteps at the nape of her neck and then a sudden tug on the fine baby hairs that grew there. "Ow! Quit it!"

"Anna?" Mrs. Lee said. Her seriously worried face was back.

"Oh, no, I mean—that's it," Anna stammered. "That's the name of the poem. 'Ow—Quit It.'"

"The poem is called 'Ow—Quit It'?" Mrs. Lee asked, folding her arms across her chest.

"Yeah," Anna said. She cleared her throat. "It goes, 'Ow—quit it . . . you're messing up my hair. Ow—quit it . . . you . . . shouldn't be back there." She smiled hopefully at her mother, who was still scrutinizing her with narrowed eyes. "It's about . . . a cat. Talking to a flea," Anna said.

"Hey—that was good," Zadie whispered.

"Thanks," Anna said. Her mother stared. "For listening, I mean. Thanks. It's . . . good practice for me. To get used to an audience, you know?"

Mrs. Lee nodded silently, and Anna held her breath. She couldn't tell if her mother was buying the whole poem thing or not.

"Well," Mrs. Lee said finally, "it's a very strange poem, but I guess your teacher wouldn't have assigned it if there weren't some value in learning it."

"Right," Anna agreed. "She wouldn't have. Mrs. Wessex is a really good teacher, and you're right. She wouldn't make me memorize a poem unless it was a good poem, and 'Ow—Quit It' is a really good poem. Really."

Zadie tugged Anna's hair again. "I have two words for you," she hissed. "Shut. Up. The more you talk, the weirder you sound."

Anna winced a little, but she managed to keep quiet.

"I see," Anna's mom said. Anna forced a smile and tried to look natural while her mother studied her face, but it was hard. She felt like an overripe piece of fruit that her mother was trying to decide how to handle. Should she throw it out or keep it for one more day?

"Well, I hate to interrupt you in the middle of your homework," Mrs. Lee said, "but quite frankly, I think you need a break. Come on—we're going to the mall."

*"The mall?"* Anna echoed.

"Yes. The mall. I need curtains for the house, and you're going to help me choose some."

"All right!" Zadie cheered from Anna's neck. "I love the mall. I hope there's a big food court. I could really go for some pizza."

"Pizza?" Anna said.

"No, we're not getting pizza," Mrs. Lee replied. "I've already started dinner. But we might be able to get a small snack—if there's time. Now get ready and meet me downstairs," she said, turning to leave.

"Yahoo! Giant pretzels, here I come!" Zadie shouted, but Anna couldn't share her enthusiasm.

"Please. Curtain shopping with my mom?" she muttered. "That's supposed to cheer me up?"

"Oh, and Anna," Mrs. Lee said, popping her head back into the room. "Do something about your hair. It's a mess."

# CHAPTER
## Six

"Ooh, these are nice," Mrs. Lee said, running her hand down the length of a set of red gingham curtains.

Anna rolled her eyes. She had thought spending the afternoon alone in her room was as lame as she could get. Now she knew she'd been wrong.

"Thanks a lot," she muttered, speaking into her jacket pocket. "Things weren't bad enough before. Good work."

Zadie poked her head out of the top of the pocket and glanced around. "Are you kidding? This is *way* better. We're at the mall!"

*Whoopee,* Anna thought.

"What do you think of these for the kitchen, Anna?" Mrs. Lee asked, still holding on to the red-checked curtains.

Anna shrugged. "I don't know," she said. "They're okay, I guess."

"Just *okay*?" her mom questioned. "I think they'd really go nicely with the black-and-white tile."

"I think you should get them," Anna said. She really didn't care what kind of curtains her mother bought. She just wanted to get out of there.

"I like them," Zadie said, but her voice sounded louder this time. Suddenly, Anna realized why.

Somehow, when she hadn't been paying attention, the tiny angel had managed to climb up onto her shoulder, where she was now perched.

"What are you doing?" Anna snapped as loudly as she could in a gritted-teeth whisper.

"Scoping out the scene," Zadie replied matter-of-factly.

"Are you *crazy*? Do you want everyone to see you?"

"Oh. Don't worry about that," Zadie said with a wave of her hand. "You're the only one who can see me. I'm invisible to everyone else."

"You're what?"

"Invisible," Zadie repeated.

Anna shook her head. "If no one else can see you, why did you have to hide on my neck and pull my hair before?"

"I don't know." Zadie shrugged. "You said 'hide,' and I guess I just forgot."

"You forgot?" Anna practically shouted.

Mrs. Lee whipped her head around. "What did you say, Anna?"

"Huh? Oh, um . . ."

"You're hot," Zadie coached her. "Tell her you're hot."

"Um, you're hot," Anna said. "I mean, *I'm* hot."

Mrs. Lee narrowed her eyes again. It was becoming her regular expression.

"Good," Zadie said. "Now tell her you need something to drink."

"You—I mean *I* need something to drink," Anna said.

Her mother sighed and placed the back of her hand to Anna's forehead. "I don't know what's gotten into you today, Anna. You're acting awfully strange. But . . . you do feel a little warm."

Anna did her best to look innocent. And hot. And to ignore the inch-and-a-half-tall person on her shoulder chanting, *"Oh, yeah, you know it, we're goin' to the food court. Oh, yeah, you know it. . . ."*

Mrs. Lee opened her pocketbook and pulled out a five-dollar bill. "Here. Go get yourself a drink and something to eat—something *healthy*—and meet me at the main entrance in . . ." She paused to check her watch. "Forty-five minutes. Okay?"

Anna nodded. "Okay."

With Zadie still cheering, Anna moved from the curtain shop—where she'd felt smothered in ugly fabric—into the bright, high-ceilinged expanse of the mall. To her surprise, she actually began to feel a little better. She walked to a planter in the center of the huge open area and stopped, looking left and then right.

"What do you think?" she said, trying not to move her lips.

Zadie stood tall and squinted in each direction. "Left. Definitely left," she said. "Trust me—I have excellent mall sense."

"Okay," Anna said, and she started down the east wing of the mall.

She had passed two shoe stores, a camera store, a candy shop, and a couple of trendy clothing stores when Zadie suddenly jumped up and started pointing.

"Oh! Let's go in there! Please, please, please, please!"

"The arcade?" Anna asked.

"Yeah! I see Storm Ranger! I play it all the time on the TruView back in my dorm room. Please—can we go play?"

Anna glanced into the dark cavern filled with blinking lights and beeping sounds. "I don't know," she said. "I've never really been all that good at video games."

"You don't have to be," Zadie said. "It's just for fun."

"Yeah, but . . ." Anna studied the crowded game room. The last time she'd been in an arcade had been with her brother. He'd played one game for a half hour on one quarter, and she'd blown through all of her money in less than fifteen minutes. It hadn't exactly been exhilarating.

"Oh, come on," said Zadie. "Just one game."

"I don't know, Zadie. Video games aren't really my—"

"Great!" the angel exclaimed. She ran down Anna's arm, speared the five-dollar bill with her wand, and ran with it—like it was a giant flag— all the way over to the change machine.

"Hey! Wait!" Anna yelled, chasing her money across the terra-cotta-tiled floor. She nearly bumped into an elderly couple and had to stop to excuse herself. Otherwise she would have caught Zadie. Unfortunately, by the time she reached the entrance to the arcade, her five-dollar bill had been turned into twenty-five golden tokens.

"Zadie! My mom's probably expecting change," Anna snapped.

"Does *she* like video games?" Zadie asked. Anna scowled at the angel and scooped up her tokens.

"Come on," Anna said, and she started to walk away.

"What?! Do you mean to tell me that you've got all those tokens and you're not even going to use one?" Zadie demanded. "You're killing me!"

Anna stopped and sighed heavily. "Fine," she said. "One game. Where is it?"

Zadie clapped and beamed. "Right there," she said, pointing to a machine surrounded by people.

"*Zadie*," Anna whined. "The line for that game is huge. We'll never get a turn."

The words were barely out of Anna's mouth when a blue light on the other side of the arcade began flashing and a loud siren started to wail.

"Someone beat Robo Warrior!" one of the boys yelled, and they all ran over to see who the new champion was.

Anna shot Zadie a sideways glance. "Okay, that was weird," she said.

Zadie just shrugged. "Game's free," she said. "Better hurry." Anna studied her small friend for another minute, then slowly—reluctantly—walked over to the newly vacated machine.

"Storm Ranger?" Anna said, raising her eyebrows.

"Yeah, kind of a lame name," Zadie admitted, "but it's really cool. See, you have to fight your way through a series of villains to get to the evil Dr. Sphere, who's turned the world into a wasteland of chaos with his SD3000 Storm Maker."

Anna frowned.

"Okay, so it *sounds* lame, too," Zadie said, "but it's really fun. I promise. Go ahead—put your tokens in."

"All right," Anna said, and she dropped two tokens into the slot. A red START GAME light began flashing, and Anna was just about to hit it when she noticed all of the other controls.

"Zadie! There are like a gazillion buttons here! I can't do this."

"Don't worry—I'll coach you," the little angel said, and she jumped on the button to start the game.

"Great. Maybe I'll last an extra ten seconds," Anna said. She grabbed the joystick with her left hand and poised her right hand above all of the colored buttons. She never understood why people wasted their money on this stuff.

"Get ready," Zadie commanded. "And three . . . two . . . one—here comes the first brute!"

As unenthusiastic as she was about the game, Anna couldn't help getting into the background music. It was a funky melody with a steady, driving beat that kept getting faster and louder as she played. In spite of herself, she felt her shoulders tense, and butterflies took over where her stomach used to be.

"Quick! Green!" Zadie yelled, and Anna smacked the green button as fast as she could.

"Great—now red! Blue! Joystick up! Now left! Yellow! Yellow! Move right! Awesome kick—do it again! And blue! You've almost got him! Red! Red! One more! Yeah!"

Zadie was jumping up and down on the screen so frantically that Anna forgot how much she hated video games and started to laugh.

"Don't get too relaxed," Zadie cautioned her. "The first guy's easy. Here comes number two!"

Anna readied herself at the controls as another enemy warrior approached. Once again

Zadie shouted out commands, and Anna executed them flawlessly until the second opponent had been reduced to dust as well.

"All *right*!" she said, a huge smile spreading across her face. Who'd have thought that crushing the cronies of chaos could be so much fun?

By the time Anna had defeated her sixth rival, Zadie had switched from yelling out specific commands to just plain yelling. Anna didn't really need advice anymore—she was doing fine on her own. What's more, she was really beginning to have fun! She didn't even mind that a few people had gathered around to watch her.

"Cool," she heard one of the onlookers say when she beat enemy number seven, and she couldn't help smiling. It felt good to be kicking butt at this game, and it didn't even matter that she was doing it alone.

"Smash him!" Zadie yelled.

Well, *almost* alone.

Finally, at the entrance to Dr. Sphere's fortress, Anna met her match. He . . . she . . . *it* was a two-legged, forty-foot-tall reptile with a plated back, twelve-inch claws, two heads, and a clubbed tail. Even Zadie wasn't sure how to tackle that one, so Anna just did what she could and at the very least went down fighting.

"Whew." Anna sighed as GAME OVER flashed on the screen. "That was fun."

"Major fun," Zadie agreed. "And you were awesome. You made it two levels farther than I ever have, and hey—look! You got your name in the top ten!"

Anna gazed down at the screen, and sure enough, it was asking her to enter her name. "Cool," Anna said. She used the joystick to choose letters until she had spelled ZADIE, then she stuck out her pinky for an angel high five.

"Thanks!" Zadie said. "Let's see where you placed." As the two of them were waiting for the screen to show the top ten high scores, Anna felt someone tap her on the shoulder.

"Hey. You're pretty good at that."

Anna turned around to see Matt Dana standing behind her. "Oh. Thanks," she said. "That was my first time."

"Whoa? Really?" he asked. Anna nodded. "Nice job. You're number six," he said, pointing at the screen. Anna turned back to see ZADIE glowing in bright green letters halfway down the list. And then she noticed the other high scores. Numbers one through five and seven through ten were all filled in with the same name: MATTYD.

"Wow. I did *okay*, but it looks like you've got me beat," she said.

Matt shrugged. "I come in here a lot," he said. "Was that really your first time playing Storm Ranger?"

"Yeah," Anna said with a laugh. "I'd never even heard of it before."

"Huh—you must be a natural," Matt said.

"Or maybe it was just beginner's luck," Anna offered. "If I play it again, I probably won't even get past the first screen."

"Maybe," Matt said, "but I doubt it. You looked like you knew what you were doing. You'll probably have all my high scores wiped out by the end of the week."

Anna jingled the tokens in her pocket. "Yeah, right. And it'll only cost me about fifty dollars."

Matt laughed. "Hey—in math class, you said something about Venice Beach. Does that mean you're from California?"

"Yeah, but not that close to Venice Beach. We just went there on weekends and stuff. I lived farther south, near San Diego."

"Cool. Were you right on the coast?"

"Mm-hm." Anna nodded.

"Ever go surfing?"

"A couple of times," Anna said. "It was a lot of fun."

"I bet. I'd love to go, but it's hard around here. The waves aren't as big, and there just aren't that many places to try."

"Yeah, my brother was pretty bummed about that when my parents told us about the move. He was really into surfing. But then I think he found some kind of East Coast surf club online, and it listed a few spots around here where the surfing is actually supposed to be okay."

"Huh. I'll have to check that out. Think you could get me the URL?"

"Sure," Anna said with a shrug.

"Cool. Meanwhile, I guess I'll just keep skateboarding."

"You skateboard?" Anna asked.

"Yeah. You?"

Anna shook her head. "No way."

"What do you mean, 'no way'? If you've surfed, you can probably skateboard. It's the same idea."

"Uh-huh. Except that if you fall off a surfboard, you land in the water. If you fall off a skateboard, you fall on the *pavement*. That's enough of a difference for me."

"So you wear pads," Matt said. "And a helmet."

"I don't know," Anna said. "I like sports that don't require body armor. You know, like eating ice cream." She grinned, pulling the gift certificate she'd won in math class out of her back pocket. "Where is Ed's, anyway?"

"It's actually here in the mall," Matt said. "And I have my certificate, too. Do you want me to show you where it is?"

"Sure," Anna said. She had just started out of the arcade behind him when she heard a tiny voice yell, "*Hel-lo?* Dreamy conversation with your new buddy, but aren't you forgetting something?"

"Oh!" Anna gasped.

"What's up?"

"I, um . . . think I left some money back there," Anna lied. She ran over to the Storm Ranger machine, scooped up the disgruntled angel, and raced back. "Just a few tokens," she said, "but I didn't want to leave them."

"That's cool," Matt said. "All set?"

"Yeah. All set," Anna said.

They walked down the mall corridors, continuing in the same direction Anna and Zadie had been heading before they found the arcade.

"Told you I had good mall sense," a muffled voice yelled from inside Anna's jacket pocket.

And after just a few more clothing stores, a giant sports place with four escalators, a coffee shop, an electronics store, and a bookseller, they hit the food court.

Zadie peeked out of Anna's pocket and started sniffing the air. "Pretzels—I smell pretzels," she said. "And pizza!" She hopped up to the top of Anna's pocket and teetered on the edge.

"Zadie—what are you doing?" Anna hissed.

"I'm busting out my beat box," the angel said. She stuck her hands under opposite armpits with her thumbs sticking out and started making percussion noises with her mouth. Then, to Anna's amazement, she started *rapping*.

> *"I wanna eat right now!*
> *When I'm at the mall, I like to chow down!*
> *My name is Zadie,*
> *They say I'm a lady,*
> *But I still know how to get crazy—"*

Anna planted her index finger on Zadie's head and pushed her back down into the pocket.

"Hey!" Zadie's muted voice protested. "I wasn't done!"

"You are now," Anna whispered.

"Fine. I get it. A human comes along and it's

bye-bye, Zadie. *Nice*. Well, I'm going to score some food—I'll meet you at the ice cream place." And with that, she jumped from Anna's pocket and ran across the floor.

Anna watched her go. She looked just like a little piece of paper being carried along by the drafts of air from people's shuffling feet. *I hope she doesn't get squished,* Anna thought. But she figured an angel who could cross from one world to another without getting injured could probably navigate the mall.

"Here it is," Matt said as he and Anna approached what looked like an old-fashioned soda shop. There was a long red counter with stainless steel sides and matching bar stools, and the three people working behind it all wore white jackets and paper hats.

"Cool," Anna said. "Do you know what you're getting?"

Matt nodded. "My usual," he said, and stepped up. "Mint chocolate chip in a plain cone, please," he said, handing over his gift certificate.

"Make that two," Anna said, presenting hers as well.

"You like mint chocolate chip?" Matt asked.

"It's my favorite," Anna said. "Back in Doncaster—that's where I lived in California—there was this ice cream place that had *green days.*"

"Green days?"

"Yeah, it was this special deal they had a few times a year—on St. Patrick's Day, the first day of spring, and . . . I guess the other one was sometime in the middle of summer or something. Anyway, on green days you could go in and get any flavor of ice cream that was green for half price. It was really cool."

"That *is* cool," Matt said.

"They did other colors, too," Anna said. "Like pink on Valentine's Day, brown whenever it was raining."

Matt scrunched his eyebrows together. "I get the pink," he said, "but what does brown have to do with rain?"

"I don't know. Maybe because rain makes mud?" Anna guessed.

"Yeah." Matt nodded. "I bet that's it." He and Anna took their ice-cream cones from the woman behind the counter, thanked her, and headed toward a table at the center of the food court. Anna licked her ice cream, pleased to find that mint chocolate chip tasted as good here as it did in California. She and Matt were just about to sit down when Anna heard someone calling Matt's name.

"Matt! Matt! Over here!"

*I know that voice,* Anna thought with a sense of dread.

"Matt! Matt Dana!" the voice called again, but Matt didn't seem to notice.

"Um . . . I think someone's trying to get your attention," Anna said.

"Huh?" Matt glanced around. "Oh." He turned in the direction of the voice and spotted Sharon Ross, waving madly. She, Kimberly, Theresa, and Carrie were sharing a table.

Matt turned back to Anna. "Do you want to sit over there?" he asked.

*No, no, a thousand times no,* Anna thought. But what was she going to say? *I can't—none of your friends like me?* Yeah, right. She might as well just tattoo an *L* on her forehead for *lame.*

"Sure," she said. She followed Matt as he made his way through the maze of tables and chairs.

"Hey, Matt," Sharon said. "It's so cool that you came for ice cream at the same time that we did. Here, have a seat." She pulled over a chair from a neighboring table and placed it next to hers. Anna looked for another seat, but no one had bothered to make room for her.

"You guys know Anna, right?" Matt said.

"Yeah," they all murmured.

"Hey, Anna—nice job on those fractions

today," Theresa said. "You really carried our team." Anna tilted her head slightly. She noticed Sharon glaring at Theresa and wasn't quite sure what to make of the whole situation. Was Theresa trying to upset Sharon? More important, was Theresa really trying to be nice to Anna, or would she just start laughing behind Anna's back again as soon as she was gone?

"Thanks," Anna said. "It really wasn't that big a deal."

"Free ice cream is a *very* big deal," Carrie disagreed, and everyone chuckled. Except Sharon. Even Kimberly was smiling until she realized Sharon wasn't amused. Again, Anna was puzzled. They didn't *seem* to hate her. Okay, so maybe Sharon did—but the others didn't.

"Hey, Anna, why don't you take that chair," Matt offered. "I'll grab another one."

It was a nice gesture, and Anna appreciated it, but the last thing she wanted was to sit next to Sharon. She looked around for another possibility, but Matt insisted. "Really. Go ahead. That's cool, right, Sharon?"

"Sure," Sharon said with a smile. Anna just about fell over.

"I'll be right back," Matt said, and he headed off in search of a chair.

"Okay," Anna said.

She glanced at Sharon. The smile vanished, and her face once again looked like it had been chiseled from stone. She had obviously wanted Matt sitting next to her, and Anna . . . well, she probably wanted Anna back on the other side of the country. But what else was there to do?

Anna swallowed hard and walked toward the chair. Maybe, just this once, Sharon would be willing to call a truce. After all, she seemed to really like Matt, and Anna had come over with him.

As Anna edged along the table to her chair, she gave Sharon a weak smile. "Bad luck on the math work sheet, huh? Those numbers were pretty blurry. I had a hard time reading some of them, too." It was a lie, but she thought it might soften Sharon up a little.

"No big deal," Sharon said with a shrug. "I've had enough free ice cream this month already."

Anna nodded. "Yeah, I heard that you usually win those—aaaaaghhhh!"

There was a bang and a thud, and suddenly, for the second time that day, Anna was on the floor. Only this time she was covered in mint chocolate chip ice cream.

"Sharon!" she heard Carrie yell.

"I didn't mean to," Sharon said.

"Did you pull out her chair?" Theresa asked.

"No—I just bumped it a little," Sharon said. "I told you she was a klutz."

"I am *not* a klutz," Anna said through gritted teeth.

"You mean you did that on purpose?" Sharon asked.

Anna looked down at her white shirt and her jeans. There were light green splotches all over them as well as on her hands and probably even her face.

"Are you okay?" Carrie asked. Anna nodded.

"Good," Kimberly said. "Because—" The corner of her mouth curved into a smirk. "I don't think I can keep from laughing much longer." And suddenly she burst out giggling, which got Sharon started, too. And it wasn't long before Theresa and Carrie had joined in.

"I'm sorry, Anna," Carrie gasped between giggles. "But you look so funny!"

Just then, Matt returned with his chair. "What happened?" he asked. The four girls were laughing so hard that no one could answer him, and Anna couldn't handle it any longer. She stood up, shook the ice cream from her hands, and hurried away.

"Anna! Wait," she heard Matt calling after her, but she wasn't stopping for anything.

"Oh, no! What happened?" a tiny voice

screeched. Anna just shook her head and kept walking. Zadie sprinted ahead, scaled a fake tree, and jumped onto Anna's shoulder as she passed by.

"I knew you were going for ice cream," Zadie said, "but I had no idea you were such a messy eater."

"I'm not," Anna said through clenched teeth. "This girl Sharon, who *hates* me, pulled my chair out from under me and I dropped my cone."

"Ooh! That's low. Which one is she?" Zadie stood on Anna's shoulder, staring back at the table where Anna had been sitting. "She's the blonde, right? Let's go get her. We'll give her a piece of your mind!"

Anna shook her head, and a few fresh drops of ice cream hit her neck. Gross. It was in her hair, too. "No. We won't," she said. "I'm through listening to you. If I had just stayed in the curtain shop with my mother, this never would have happened. I'm covered in ice cream, I feel like an idiot, and I want to go home."

"Yeah, but you can't just let her get away with that," Zadie protested.

"I can, and I did," Anna said. "If you want to go find her and tell her off, be my guest. But you're on your own. I'm outta here."

# CHAPTER
## Seven

"Sorry," said the boy behind Anna in the lunch line. He and his friends—a few seventh graders—were horsing around, and one of them had pushed him into her.

"It's okay," Anna murmured. At least she was still standing—for once. But Anna wasn't about to let her guard down, even though it had been a pretty uneventful day. So far.

She hadn't been tripped, knocked over, or publicly humiliated, although she had heard Sharon saying something about how she'd never be able to eat mint chocolate chip ice cream again. But no one else had said a word.

At one point, during English class, she thought she saw Carrie and Theresa trying to get her attention, but Anna had refused to look their way. They had probably just wanted to laugh at her some more.

The lunch line moved forward, and Anna reached for a tray from the shining silver cart. As she did, she felt the brown paper lunch sack she was holding in her other hand begin to tear. Thankfully, she managed to set it on the tray before the whole thing split open, scattering whatever her mother had packed for her everywhere.

"That was lucky," she muttered to herself. "Maybe I'm finally going to have a day where nothing goes wrong."

"Phew! At last, some fresh air!" a familiar voice squeaked. *Or not.*

"Oh, no," Anna groaned. She glanced down to see Zadie peeking out through the hole in the paper bag. "What are you doing here?"

"Nice to see you, too," Zadie said. She crawled out of the sack and jumped down to Anna's lunch tray. "Hey," she said, sniffing twice. "Something smells good. What's for lunch?"

"You're *always* hungry, aren't you?" Anna murmured. "It's pizza, but I'm just getting fries. My mom packed my lunch."

"Yeah, I know," Zadie said, wincing. "I've been hanging out with it all morning. *Tuna.* Ick. You should definitely get the pizza."

"Whatever," Anna muttered. "How'd you get in there, anyway?"

"Well, after you refused to bring me to school with you," Zadie sneered, "I sneaked down to the kitchen and jumped into your lunch bag when your mom wasn't looking."

Anna slid her tray along the metal counter. "Why?" she asked. "Why couldn't you just stay home like I told you?"

"Because you need me," Zadie said. "And you need a slice of that pizza, too. Make it pepperoni, 'kay?" Anna shook her head, but she did order the pizza. Tuna wasn't exactly her favorite, either.

"All right," Zadie said, scurrying up Anna's arm. "You do the lunch line thing, I'll find us a seat. Hmmm . . ." Zadie scanned the cafeteria from her perch on Anna's shoulder.

"Definitely not at that table," she said. "Too many teachers, and you don't want to look like a brownnoser. And you can't sit over there, either, because it looks like those older girls are saving all the seats. Huh. This isn't easy, is it?"

"Tell me about it," Anna said. "I usually just sit at that little table in the back corner."

Zadie checked it out. "Okay, two things: First, there's no way you're sitting alone today.

And second, you're getting really good at talking without moving your lips. Have you considered becoming a ventriloquist?"

"Oh, yeah. That would send my popularity rating through the roof," Anna scoffed.

"It's just a thought," Zadie said. Then she did a little jump. "Ooh! I've got it. See that table over there—third one back? That's where we're sitting today."

Anna set some fries on her tray, then moved into line at the cash register. "Third one back?" she repeated, searching for the table Zadie had chosen. "Are you kidding?" she said when she spotted it.

One side of the long, rectangular table was packed with girls—among them Carrie, Theresa, Kimberly, and Sharon. On the other side of the table was a group of boys, including Matt Dana. In the middle were plenty of spare seats, but Anna had no intention of sitting in one of them.

"It's okay," Zadie said. "The seats are attached to the table. There's no way anyone could pull yours out—I already checked."

"Forget it," Anna said, moving forward in line. "If I go over there, Sharon will do something to make me look stupid, and I'm not going to set myself up for that."

"What if Sharon left?" Zadie asked.

"She's not going to leave," Anna said. "She's eating lunch."

"Yeah, but what if she did leave?" Zadie persisted. "Then would you go over there?"

Anna scowled at the angel. She was really becoming an annoyance. "Sure," Anna said. "If Sharon just got up and left, sure. Why not? I'd run right over and make friends with the whole darned table. But she's *not* leaving."

"We'll see about that," Zadie said. Anna just rolled her eyes. *Tomorrow I'm locking her in my jewelry box,* she thought.

Anna paid the cashier and waited for her change. Meanwhile, Zadie was dancing around on her shoulder, waving her wand and chanting something that sounded like:

*Heckle, deckle, pickled ear,*
*Now make Sharon disappear!*

She circled her wand in the air twice and pointed it in Sharon's direction. Nothing happened.

"Shoot me now," Anna muttered.

"What's that, honey?" the cashier asked.

"Oh. Nothing," Anna said, taking her change. "Just—thanks."

"I don't get it," Zadie said. "That should

have worked." Anna grabbed a small paper cup and began filling it with ketchup. "Shoot!" Zadie exclaimed, examining the ball at the tip of her wand. "That's the problem. It was set on *Ask again later.*"

Anna squinted at the tiny wand. "Oh, my gosh," she said, eyeing the tiny sphere. "Is that a Magic 8-Ball?"

"Yeah—isn't it great?" Zadie asked. "Kind of hip, kind of retro. And it works really well, too—when it's set right." She shook her wand and checked the message in the transparent window of the Magic 8-Ball. "*It is doubtful,*" she read. "That won't work."

Zadie jiggled the wand again and came up with *Don't count on it.* "Darned thing," she muttered, giving it another shake. "Ha! There. *Signs point to yes.* That'll do it."

She started her crazy dance again and yelled out another spell:

*The second try will save the day.*
*Now make Sharon go away!*

Again she circled the wand above her head and thrust it toward Sharon. Again nothing happened.

"Zadie," Anna sighed. "Couldn't you just—"

"Please excuse the interruption," a voice said

over the intercom. "Could Sharon Ross please come to the office. That's Sharon Ross to the office. Thank you."

Anna's jaw dropped. If her tray hadn't been resting on the condiment table, it probably would have dropped, too. She watched as Sharon got up and left the cafeteria. Then she stared at Zadie.

"Told you it would work," the angel said with a smug smile. "Now, go on. Sit down."

Slowly, Anna picked up her tray and began walking toward the table. But the closer she got, the worse her stomach felt. "I . . . *can't.*"

Zadie groaned. "Fine. Have it your way. Go sit at that little table, all alone."

Anna knew the angel was disgusted with her, but she just couldn't bring herself to sit with the others. What if they started laughing at her again?

She quickened her pace, determined to walk by before anyone saw her, but unfortunately, she didn't speed up quite enough. Just as she was passing the table where Matt and the others were seated, Zadie grabbed a fry and chucked it—like a javelin—right at Matt Dana's head.

"Hey," he said when it hit him on the cheek.

He looked up, trying to determine where the renegade fry had come from, but the only person nearby was Anna.

"Anna!" he called. "Over here."

Anna stopped dead. "Tomorrow you're staying home," she hissed at Zadie. Reluctantly, she walked over to Matt's table.

"Hi," she said quietly. She was just about to apologize for the fry when he broke in.

"Hey, Ryan," he said to one of the other boys. "This is Anna. The one who made it to level nine on Storm Ranger yesterday."

"Cool," Ryan said. "You must play a lot. The farthest I've ever made it is level seven."

Anna straightened up. "Actually, it was my first time," she said.

"No way!" another boy exclaimed.

"Are you serious?" Ryan asked.

"Yeah," Anna said. "But like I told Matt—I probably just got lucky, you know? I mean, I doubt I could ever do it again."

"Wow," a few of the guys said. Anna smiled, remembering how it had felt to get so far in that game in front of all those people. She really had done well, hadn't she? And she still had twenty-three tokens to use. Maybe she would wipe out a few of Matt's high scores after all.

"Hey," Matt said, interrupting her thoughts. "Where are you sitting?"

"Ummm . . ." Anna hesitated. She didn't exactly want to admit that she was planning to sit alone.

"Because there's plenty of room here," Matt offered, nodding toward the empty seats.

"Oh. Uh . . . okay," Anna said. She couldn't help wondering why he was being so nice to her.

"Maybe he thinks you're cool, or maybe he's just a nice guy," Zadie said, reading her mind. "Who cares? Just sit down."

Anna took the angel's advice and set her tray down next to Matt's. As she did, Carrie and Theresa both looked over.

"Hi, Anna," Theresa called. She raised her hand to wave and accidentally knocked over her juice glass. "Oops," she said, standing it up again quickly. A bit of punch had spilled on her cookie, but that was all. "See—you shouldn't worry about the ice cream," Theresa told her. "I'm always doing stuff like that. *Without* Sharon's help," she added.

"Yeah." Carrie laughed.

Anna blinked rapidly. Did that mean Theresa and Carrie knew that Sharon had been lying and that she really *had* pulled out Anna's chair? She looked over at their smiling faces and felt a sense of relief. Maybe there was a chance the three of them could be friends after all.

"So, Anna, what did you think of the Toxic Ogre?" Matt asked as she took her seat. "You know—the one right outside Dr. Sphere's fortress?"

"Oh, right," Anna said. "He was creepy. Didn't he have two heads?"

"Yeah—that's because of the mutation," Ryan put in.

"The *mutation*?" Anna said with a giggle, and the boys began to give her the lowdown on the game. They told her some of the same stuff Zadie had already mentioned, but they also had a lot of other information. In fact, they actually made the game seem even more interesting.

Anna was so into the conversation that she didn't even notice when Sharon walked back in. Until she spoke.

"Can you believe it?" Sharon said. "There wasn't even a message. They said the announcement must have been a mistake."

"Whoa—wicked witch at three o'clock," Zadie chirped. Anna tensed a little. She tried to focus on Matt, Ryan, and the others as they described more of the villains, but she kept one eye and one ear on Sharon, too. Just in case.

"That's weird," Kimberly said.

"Hey, what's she doing here?" Sharon said, and Anna didn't need three guesses to figure out who she was talking about. "This is *our* table," Sharon went on. "She can't just—"

"Matt invited her," Carrie broke in.

"And if he hadn't, we were going to," Theresa added. "Carrie and I think she's nice." Anna could hardly believe her ears. Were they actually standing up to Sharon? *For her?* It certainly sounded that way. And to Anna's surprise, it seemed to be working. Sharon sat back down and started eating without another word. And only *one* death glare.

*This must be my lucky day,* Anna thought. She reached into the paper bag her mother had packed for her. The sandwich might be tuna, but there was usually something yummy for dessert. Anna grabbed a small, square plastic container and pulled it out to reveal chocolate . . . crumbs.

"Oh, yeah," Zadie said. "I meant to tell you—your mom makes *awesome* brownies. Let's snag some more when we get home. And hey— how about sharing some of that pizza?"

# CHAPTER
# Eight

"Matt! Over here," Jeremy Gray shouted.

Anna watched as Matt kicked the soccer ball to Jeremy, who dribbled it a few feet before crossing it back. Then wham! Matt took a perfect shot, and the ball went soaring right into the net.

"Nice one, Matt," Ryan said, giving him a high five. Anna was impressed, too. It seemed like Matt was good at everything. Math, video games, sports. And it was becoming more and more obvious that he was really popular, too.

At first, Anna had pegged him as a bit of a loner, and in a way, he was. He didn't seem to care much about what other people thought, and he clearly liked to hang out alone from time to time—like yesterday, at the arcade. But it was also clear that he had plenty of people to hang out with if he wanted.

Plus, even though he was kind of quiet, whenever he *did* talk, everyone listened—Sharon Ross in particular.

"Okay, everybody," Ms. Gilbert said. "Let's count off by twos."

When everyone was done, she ordered the twos to one side of the field and the ones to the other. Anna, who was a two, was glad to see that she had ended up on Matt's team.

"Anna—cool," he said as she walked over. "Are you as good at soccer as you are at video games?"

"Not even," Anna said. And she wasn't kidding. Gym had always been her least favorite class, unless they were playing games like dodgeball— she was pretty good at stuff like that. But soccer? Forget about it. She'd rather have answered her mother's embarrassing preteen questions.

"Don't worry," Matt said. "I'll set you up."

"What about me?" Sharon said. "I'm on your team, too. Will you pass me the ball?"

"Oh, hey, Sharon," Matt said. "Yeah. Sure."

"Cool," Sharon said, "because I was the high scorer on my traveling team, you know. All you have to do is cross it to me just outside the circle and I guarantee I'll get it in."

"All right," Matt said, but he didn't actually sound all that impressed.

"Anna," Sharon said, touching Anna's forearm like they were old friends, "I never got to talk to you after you fell and spilled ice cream all over yourself yesterday. Are you okay?"

Anna narrowed her eyes. What was this about? "Yeah, I'm fine," she said.

"I'm really sorry for laughing," Sharon said. "You just looked so funny. I hope you can forgive me."

"Uhhh . . ." Anna felt like she was in the twilight zone. Sharon Ross, asking for forgiveness? Please.

Before Anna could answer, Ms. Gilbert blew her whistle. "Everybody on Matt Dana's team grab a red pinny. Jeremy's team will be blue. Let's go!"

Anna took the opportunity to break away from Sharon and her freaky personality disorder, but Sharon barely even noticed. She was already talking Matt's ear off.

*Well, that was bizarre,* Anna thought. She reached into the mesh bag and grabbed her red pinny. She was about to walk away when she spotted Zadie, reclining in a miniature lawn chair on the sideline.

"Knock 'em dead," she said, raising a candy bar in the air.

"Where did you get that?" Anna asked, but Zadie just shrugged.

"How's the Wicked Witch of the West?" she asked.

"Weird," Anna answered. "She's acting all nice to impress Matt Dana."

"Is it working?"

Anna squinted. "I don't think so."

"Yahoo!" cheered Zadie. "Score one for the nice guys!"

"*Zadie,*" Anna chastised.

"Hey, Anna," Theresa called as she and Carrie bounded over. "Are you a two?"

"Yeah," Anna replied.

"Cool, so are we," Carrie said.

Anna smiled. "Awesome." She was psyched to be playing with Matt, but she was even more psyched to be on a team with Carrie and Theresa. The three of them had sat together in math class again—Matt had sat with Ryan and Jeremy instead—and Anna had really enjoyed talking with them. They were nice and funny, and they actually seemed to like her.

The only drawback was that Sharon had spent more time than usual glaring at her, and somehow her glares had felt more intense. In fact, it seemed to Anna that the more she,

Carrie, and Theresa laughed, the angrier Sharon looked.

Anna had just pulled her pinny over her head when Ms. Gilbert blew her whistle and told the teams to set up. In another minute, she blew her whistle again, and the game began.

"Go, Anna, go! Go, Anna, go!" Zadie cheered from the sideline.

Matt had put Anna at center forward. It made Anna a little nervous, but he seemed to think she could handle it. Matt was playing the left wing, and Sharon had put herself in as the right.

"Now, Anna! Go through!" Matt yelled. Anna wasn't sure, but she assumed he meant for her to run toward the goal.

She did, watching as Matt took the ball down the side, dribbling the ball past one defender and then another. When he was about twenty yards out, he crossed the ball and yelled for Anna to shoot it.

Anna could hardly believe he had passed it to *her*. He really seemed to think she could handle it, and strangely, Anna was beginning to think so, too. She ran at the ball as fast as she could and kicked it. Whoosh! It went right into the net.

"I thought you said you couldn't play," Matt said, running over to slap her hand.

"I didn't think I could." Anna laughed.

"Nice one, Anna!" Carrie yelled, and she gave her a high five, too.

As Anna jogged back to the center of the field, she felt lighter than she had in days. Things were finally going her way, and it felt great.

"Lucky shot," Sharon sneered as she ran past Anna. "I'd like to see you try it again."

"Maybe I will," Anna said.

Sharon stopped and faced her. "What did you say?"

"I said . . . maybe I will," Anna repeated, but somehow it lacked the boldness it'd had the first time.

"Go for it," Sharon said, and she trotted back to her position. There was something about the way she had spoken the words that chilled Anna, but she tried to let it go. She'd just scored a goal, and Matt Dana believed in her. What could Sharon possibly do?

On the next play, Jeremy's team started with the ball. At one point, it looked like Jeremy might score, but Theresa managed to steal the ball away.

"Theresa—over here!" Sharon called, and Theresa passed her the ball. To Anna's surprise, Sharon was almost as impressive as Matt Dana.

She went through three opponents without much trouble and probably could have driven all the way to the goal. Instead, she called to Anna.

"Lee! This one's all yours!" she yelled, and she gave the ball a serious kick—straight into a huge puddle that splashed all over Anna, drenching her from head to toe.

"Yuck!" Anna shouted, wiping a huge glob of mud off her face. Laughter erupted all over the field, and Ms. Gilbert blew her whistle.

"All right, people—it's just mud. Play on!"

She blew her whistle again, and Sharon ran over to the ball. "Don't worry, I'll take it from here, Anna," she called, dribbling toward the goal. "Bad luck about that mud puddle, huh?"

*Yeah, right. Bad luck,* Anna thought. And something told her that she was going to keep right on having bad luck as long as Sharon Ross was around.

# CHAPTER
## Nine

"Girls," Mrs. Wessex called, interrupting Theresa midstory. She'd been telling Carrie and Anna about the time she'd knocked over an entire display of soda cans in the grocery store. "Back to work, please."

Carrie's face went red. She hunched over her drawing of King Tut's tomb and began coloring diligently. Theresa shrugged and started scanning the encyclopedia for more information about the process of mummification.

"Sheesh," Anna muttered. "I don't know why they call this class *social* studies if they're never going to let us talk." In spite of Mrs. Wessex's watchful eye, both Carrie and Theresa giggled. And thankfully, the bell rang before they could get into trouble for it.

"You're so funny, Anna," Theresa said as

they walked to their lockers. Anna grinned. In spite of Sharon's little stunt in gym class, this had been her best day yet.

"Hey—do you guys want to come over this afternoon?" she asked. "My house is still full of boxes and stuff, but my grandmother said she was going to make honey cakes today."

"Honey cakes?" Theresa asked.

"Yeah, they're sort of like pancakes, but sweeter and crispier. I guess she used to make them all the time when she lived in Korea. They're *really* good."

"Did your grandmother grow up in Korea?" Carrie asked.

"Mm-hmm." Anna nodded. "She moved to the United States right before my mom was born."

"Wow—that's cool," Carrie said. "And she lives with you?"

"Yep. So do you want to come over?" Anna asked again.

Carrie lowered her eyes. "Oh, um . . ." She stared down at her feet, then shot Theresa a nervous glance.

"The thing is—" Theresa started.

Suddenly—and without warning—Sharon burst into the conversation. "Are you guys ready?" she asked. "My mom said she'd be here right at three."

Anna tried to make eye contact with Theresa and Carrie, but neither one of them would look at her.

"Oh, hi, Anna," Sharon added as an after-thought. "Carrie, Theresa, Kimberly, and I are going to the movies. What are *you* doing this afternoon?"

"Uhhh—"

"Maybe you could come with us?" Theresa suggested, brightening.

"Yeah," Carrie said. She looked hopefully at Sharon.

"Sorry," Sharon said. "There's only room for four in my mom's van—the back is full of sports equipment."

"Oh," Theresa said, slouching. She and Carrie seemed genuinely disappointed. Sharon, on the other hand, was smirking—but only when Theresa and Carrie weren't watching.

"That's okay," Anna said. "I have a lot of stuff to do, anyway. I'm still unpacking and everything."

"Huh. That sounds like fun," Sharon said. Then she turned to Carrie and Theresa. "Come on, guys—let's go," she said.

"Okay," Carrie said. "I just have to grab my jacket."

"Me, too," Theresa added. "Bye, Anna. See you tomorrow."

"Yeah. See you tomorrow," Anna agreed. She went to her locker and packed up her things, trying not to pay attention as Sharon, Carrie, Theresa, and Kimberly walked out, laughing and talking about how good the movie was going to be.

"No room in her mom's van," Anna muttered to herself. "Yeah. I bet." There could have been seating for fifty and Sharon still would have found a way to exclude her. She was never going to have anyone to hang out with if Sharon had her way, and something told her that Sharon got her way most of the time.

Anna put on her backpack and started down the sidewalk toward home. Things had been going so well with Theresa and Carrie. Why did Sharon always have to come along and mess things up?

"And why does she have it in for me?" Anna wondered aloud.

"Because you're cool!" a tiny voice yelled. "Haven't you figured that out yet?" Anna glanced down to see Zadie cruising up on a miniature motor scooter.

"Where are you getting all this stuff?" Anna demanded. "Angels R Us?"

"Ha! Good one." Zadie laughed.

"And what do you mean, I'm cool?" Anna added. "I thought we went over that already. If I were cool, I wouldn't be spending the afternoon cleaning my room. If I were cool, I'd have friends to hang out with. I don't, and I'm not. Got it?"

Anna sped up her pace.

Zadie sped up her scooter. "*I* had it a long time ago," she yelled over the sound of her engine. It sounded like a buzzing mosquito. "*You're* the one who doesn't get it. Whoa! Cute guy, six o'clock! I'll see you at home!"

"Cute guy, what?" Anna asked.

"Hey, Anna—wait," a voice called. Anna turned to see Matt Dana approaching on his skateboard. "What's up?" he asked when he was a little closer.

Anna snorted. "I'm going home to clean my room," she said. "Doesn't that sound like fun?"

"About as fun as helping my dad clean the garage," Matt said with a laugh. He rode alongside as Anna walked, coasting ahead on his skateboard every once in a while and then looping back to stay even with her. A few times he hopped his board up onto the curb and back down again without falling.

"You're pretty good at that," Anna said.

"Lots of practice," Matt replied. He built up speed, then jumped off the curb, twirling the board beneath him, and just missed the landing. "Still need more, though," he added. "You want to try?"

"No way." Anna laughed. "I prefer water to pavement, remember? Fewer injuries."

Matt grinned. "You wouldn't get injured," he said. "You might bruise your shins or scrape your elbows or something, but nothing serious."

"Oh, is that all?" Anna joked. "Well, then— bring on the ramps."

"Actually, I have a few ramps in my backyard."

"No way," Anna said.

"Yeah. And my brother and I are building a half-pipe, too. I've been sketching out the plans for it in school."

"You draw?" Anna asked.

"Sort of," Matt said. "I like to sketch things. And I doodle a lot in class."

Anna chuckled. "That explains why you're always sharpening your pencils."

"Yeah, they wear out pretty quick. Plus, I hate to sit still for too long, and sharpening pencils is a good excuse to move around."

"And knock people over," Anna added.

"Oh, yeah. Sorry about that," Matt said. "I really didn't mean to, you know."

"I know. It's okay. Besides, you already apologized."

Matt nodded, then he rode up ahead on his skateboard and tried the twirling thing again. This time he landed it, and Anna clapped.

"All right! That was cool!" she said.

Matt glided back to her and stopped, kicking the board into the air and catching it. "Say the word and I'll give you your first lesson."

"I'll think about it," Anna said. "But I'm not sure I'm ready for the half-pipe."

Anna and Matt walked for a while without talking, and Anna began to realize that even though Carrie and Theresa had taken off with Sharon, she still wasn't alone. Matt was actually becoming a pretty good friend to her, and Sharon didn't seem to have nearly as much influence over him. Maybe he'd want to hang out sometime. They could go to the arcade and play Storm Ranger or something.

Just then, a minivan drove by, and someone yelled out, "Anna's got a boyfriend!" It was Kimberly Price, and as the van passed, Anna saw Sharon drawing a big heart on the fogged-up rear window. She didn't need binoculars to know whose initials were going inside.

Anna turned to Matt, who was scraping mud off the wheels of his skateboard.

"Wasn't that Sharon's car?" he asked. "Did someone yell something to you?"

Anna was relieved that he hadn't understood Kimberly's singsong voice, but it didn't stop her from blushing bright pink. "I—I don't know," she stammered.

"Huh. Weird," Matt said, hopping back on his skateboard.

"Yeah," Anna agreed, but all she could think was, *What if he* had *heard?* Would he think that she really did like him? That she wanted him to be her boyfriend? And if so, what would he think of her then?

*He'd probably think I was a major loser,* Anna thought. After all, he didn't seem to like the way Sharon fawned over him. If anything, he preferred the comfortable friendship he and Anna were developing. And she didn't want to lose that.

But if Kimberly and Sharon started teasing her about him on a regular basis—or worse yet, telling him that she liked him—he was bound to get uncomfortable. And then he'd stop hanging around her altogether, which would leave Anna alone, again—just the way Sharon wanted her.

# CHAPTER
## Ten

"It's like she doesn't want me to have any friends at all!" Anna said.

"Sharon wasn't the one who yelled," Zadie pointed out. "Kimberly was."

"Yeah, but Kimberly doesn't even breathe unless Sharon tells her to," Anna said. "And besides, Sharon was drawing the heart."

Anna flopped down on her bed next to the angel. "Why does she hate me so much? Why doesn't she want anyone to like me?"

Zadie lay back on a tiny pillow she had placed on top of Anna's pillow and put her arms behind her head. "I already gave you that answer."

"Oh, right. *Because I'm cool,*" Anna scoffed. "Good one."

"It's true," Zadie said. She pulled a bag of

potato chips from out of nowhere and split open the top. "If you weren't a threat, she wouldn't care."

"What are you talking about?" Anna said. "How am *I* a threat to Sharon Ross?"

"Who won the last math contest?" Zadie asked, popping a chip into her mouth.

Anna scowled at her. "What does that have to do with it?"

"Sheesh. How can somebody so smart be so dumb?" Zadie muttered. "Just answer me. Who won the last math contest?"

"I did—with Carrie, Theresa, and Matt."

"Right," Zadie said. "And who won all of the math contests *before* you showed up?"

Anna shrugged. "Sharon and whatever team she was on, I guess."

"Right again," Zadie congratulated her. "Now, who won the mock spelling bee in English class last week?"

"*Zadie,*" Anna said, rolling her eyes.

"Just answer," the angel commanded, crunching another potato chip.

Anna sighed. "I did."

"Very good. And who do you think used to win all the mock spelling bees before you showed up?"

"How would I know?" Anna asked.

Zadie folded her arms and frowned. "Take a guess."

"Sharon?"

"Bingo! Question number three: Who are Sharon's best friends—besides Kimberly Price?"

Anna rolled her eyes. "Carrie and Theresa?" she guessed.

"Right again! And who do they really seem to be warming up to?"

*"Warming up to?"* Anna echoed. "You sound like my mother."

"I'm sorry—the answer is Anna Lee," Zadie announced. "Question four: What boy in the fifth grade does Sharon seem to have a little crush on?" Zadie continued.

"Zadie, what are you trying to—"

"Never mind," Zadie interrupted. "I'll answer that one for you: Matt Dana! And question number five: Who's been paying an awful lot of attention to you lately?"

Anna exhaled heavily. "Okay, I get the—"

"Matt Dana!" Zadie yelled, answering her own question again. "Jim, tell the lady what she's won."

"Cut it out, Zadie," Anna said. "I get the point. Okay. So maybe, in some small, strange way, Sharon might see me as a threat. But what am I supposed to do about it? Act dumb and stay friendless?"

"Well, you've already got half of it down."

"Zadie!"

"Sorry—bad joke," Zadie said.

Anna shook her head. "No, it's not," she said. "That's the problem. It's not a joke—it's the truth. I *am* friendless. And as long as Sharon keeps picking on me, I'm going to stay that way."

"So make her stop."

Anna hit her forehead. "What a great idea! Why didn't I think of that?"

"There's that attitude." Zadie frowned. She pointed her tiny index finger at Anna. "What you need to do is start using it for good—not evil."

"*Good, not evil?* Who am I, Wonder Woman?"

"No, but you're quick—and you know what I mean," Zadie said. "You have to start using your attitude to help yourself—not hurt yourself."

Anna groaned. "I don't have the slightest clue what you're talking about."

"Fine," Zadie said. She stood up and brushed the potato chip crumbs from her skirt. "I was hoping I wouldn't have to go this far, but it looks like I'm going to have to do the whole Ghost of Christmas Past thing."

"The whole what?"

"Ghost of Christmas Past," Zadie repeated. "You know—Charles Dickens? *A Christmas Carol*?" Anna gave her a blank stare. "Never mind. It's not important," Zadie said, jumping onto Anna's shoulder. "Just hang on."

"Why? Where are we—?"

Before Anna could finish her sentence, a gray mist formed in her room, and the next thing she knew, she was floating.

"Zadie—what's going on? Where are we?" Anna asked. Then suddenly, the mist began to dissolve and the scene became clear. They were in a large room filled with round tables and bright orange chairs.

"Jackson Intermediate!" Anna shouted. "And there's Mr. Metcalf! He was my homeroom teacher."

Just then, a bell rang, and five seconds later the cafeteria flooded with students. "Oh, wow!" Anna exclaimed. "There's Kristen . . . and Claire. And that's Hannah Galloway—she always had the best birthday parties. And there are Ian and Evan—they're twins, and they're so funny. And—oh, my gosh! Caitlin! Leah!" Anna yelled as her two best friends walked in.

She tried to run over to them, but Zadie stopped her. "They can't hear you or see you. We're just here to observe."

Anna sighed. "Still," she said, "it's so good to see them. I wish I could be back here for real. Then I wouldn't have to worry about people picking on me and making me look stupid."

"Shhh." Zadie put her finger to her lips. "Let's see what they're talking about."

In an instant, Anna found herself standing directly behind her friends in the lunch line. She was so close, she could have touched them, but they seemed to look right past her.

"That was so great when you told Jeff off at recess!" Leah gushed. "I still can't believe you did it."

"Neither can I," Caitlin said. "But I was just *so* mad. I mean, that was like the fifth time someone came up to me and asked me if I was his girlfriend. He must have been telling everyone that we were going out—just because my mom gives him a ride to school."

"What a creep," Leah said. "The best part was when you told him the only time you'd ever go out with him was in his dreams and your nightmares. What a great line!"

"Oh, that *is* good," Anna whispered to Zadie.

"Yeah, too bad I didn't make it up," Caitlin said.

Leah crinkled her nose. "You didn't?"

"No. I stole it from Anna, remember? She used it that time John Chase claimed she had given him that really mushy valentine."

"That's right!" Leah said. "Oh, my gosh, that was so perfect. I can almost hear her saying it: 'In your dreams and my nightmares, Chase,'" Leah mimicked.

"Huh. I'd almost forgotten about that," Anna told Zadie. "That was in fourth grade."

"Wow. She had some really great lines, didn't she?" Leah said.

Caitlin smiled. "Yeah. She was fast."

The two girls moved up to the front of the lunch line and grabbed their trays. Anna and Zadie moved with them.

"See?" Zadie said. "You *used* to use your attitude to put people in their place."

Anna shrugged. "I did it one time, Zadie. And it was over a year ago," she replied. "That doesn't prove anything."

Caitlin and Leah each grabbed a milk from the cooler and started along the buffet tables. When they got to the pizza, they each took a slice, and then Leah turned excitedly to Caitlin.

"Hey—do you remember that time we were at the mall and Allison Sanchez started making fun of Anna in front of everybody?" she asked.

"Uh-huh." Caitlin nodded. "She said Anna was so little, she looked like a second grader, and a strong wind would probably blow her away."

"Right," Leah said. "And do you remember what Anna said?"

Caitlin thought it over for a minute, then started to giggle. "She said, 'I'd rather be small and quick than big and dumb.'"

"Right, and Allison was ripped! She said, 'Hey—who are you calling dumb?'"

"And Anna said, 'Jeez, if you can't figure that out, it's worse than I thought.'"

"The look on Allison's face!" Leah exclaimed.

Both girls giggled, and Anna chuckled, too. "That *was* pretty good," she mused. "And Allison never teased me again." She glanced at Zadie, who was standing on her shoulder . . . *nibbling her own slice of pizza*. "Hey—where'd you get that?" Anna asked.

"Shhh! It's not important," Zadie told her. "Keep listening."

"But you know what my favorite Anna Lee line was?" Caitlin asked.

"What?" Anna and Leah said at the same time.

"It was that time Josh Hallett told Robin LaRue that she couldn't be on his kickball team at recess because they were having an all-guys' game," Caitlin said. "Remember that?"

"Oh, yeah," Leah said, "and Robin was really upset."

"Mm-hmm. So Anna marched right out to the middle of the field, where he was pitching, and she went up one side of him and down the other," Caitlin said. "She called him a—"

"*Deleterious gynophobe,*" Leah put in.

"Yeah, that was it," Caitlin agreed. "And Josh said, 'What's that supposed to mean?' So Anna said, 'I'll tell you what—you go look it up. We're going to play kickball.'"

"Right." Leah giggled. "And then she yelled out, 'Girls against the guys!' and we all ran out to play."

"And we won!" Caitlin said.

"That was the best ever," Leah said. "I miss her."

"I miss you, too," Anna said. She tried to touch Leah's shoulder, but suddenly the gray mist was back. And before she knew it, she and Zadie were back in her bedroom at the new house. In Newcastle.

"Okay—so what'd you learn?" Zadie asked,

popping one last bite of pizza into her mouth.

"That I miss Doncaster," Anna said with a sigh. "And my old school, and my old friends."

"Anything else?" Zadie asked.

Anna shrugged. "I don't know. Not really."

"Not really?" Zadie screeched. "What's wrong with you?!" She started pacing up and down Anna's pillow, shaking her head and muttering. "Humans are *so* thick. The next time I have to come back here, I want to work with a different species. Do you hear me?" she yelled up at the ceiling.

"All right," Zadie went on, taking a deep breath. "Let's go over this one more time. Ready?" She gazed at Anna expectantly.

"Sure," Anna said.

"Okay. You grew up in Doncaster, right?"

"Right."

"And somehow you managed to make some pretty good friends there, right?"

Anna nodded. "Right."

"Phew—so far, so good," Zadie said. "Now—back in Doncaster, people also used to pick on you from time to time, right?"

"I guess," Anna said.

"But back in Doncaster, you used to stand up for yourself, didn't you?"

"I don't know," Anna said. "Kind of, I guess."

"No—not *kind of*," Zadie corrected. "You did. That's what your friends were just talking about—how good you were at putting people in their place."

"So?" Anna said.

"So . . . what happened?"

Anna flopped down on her bed. "We moved, that's what happened."

"Oh, I see," Zadie said. "And what—the airline lost your spine? You left it behind, in the corner of your old closet?"

"*Zadie*," Anna moaned.

"No, really—I want to know," the angel insisted. "Where is it? You used to have one. Maybe it's in that box over there," she said, pointing her wand toward the box on top of Anna's bureau. "Maybe you just haven't unpacked it yet."

"Come on, Zadie—don't you get it? Things are different here. I had friends to back me up in Doncaster."

"You have people who want to be your friends here," Zadie countered.

"Yeah, but Sharon Ross is never going to let that happen," Anna said.

"Sharon Ross has nothing to do with it."

Anna clicked her tongue. "How can you say that? She picks on me all the time and makes me look like a great big doofus!"

"Only because you let her," Zadie said.

"I don't *let* her," Anna yelled. "She just does it."

Zadie shook her head. "John Chase tried to do it, but you didn't let him."

"That was different," Anna said.

"Allison Sanchez tried to do it, but you didn't let her, either. And Josh Hallett tried to do it to one of your friends, but you stopped him."

"Yeah." Anna sighed. "But here it's—"

"Different?" Zadie asked. "No, it's not. What's different is that you keep letting Sharon get away with it. You haven't even tried to stand up for yourself. Not once."

Anna propped herself up on her elbows and rested her chin on her hands. "I haven't, have I?" she said quietly. "Still . . . what's the point now? It's too late. Sharon's already made me look like a fool."

"Mm-hmm, and she's going to keep right on doing it if you keep making it so easy for her."

Anna closed her eyes. Zadie was right. Sharon had been bullying her since her first day of school, and she wasn't ever going to stop unless Anna made her.

"You're right," Anna said finally, looking at Zadie. "But . . . how am I supposed to stop her? Spill ice cream all over *her*? I couldn't do something like that."

"You don't need to," Zadie said. "All you have to do is be yourself. Use that attitude of yours to turn things around."

"I don't know, Zadie," Anna said. "It sounds so easy, but . . ."

"All right—one more thing. Remember this: No one can make you feel like a fool without your help. *So don't help her.* Got it?"

Anna sighed again. "Yeah. I think so," she said. Still, she couldn't help wishing that Zadie could just magically transport her back to Doncaster for good. Going back seemed like it would be so much easier than moving forward.

# CHAPTER
## Eleven

The next day in English, Anna tried to focus on her compound-verb work sheet, but she couldn't stop thinking about what Zadie had said. No one could make her feel like a fool without her help. It was really beginning to make sense.

After Matt Dana had knocked her over in this class, all Sharon had done was laugh—and make a rude comment later in the hallway. But really, what was the big deal? No one seemed to think any less of Matt, and he was the one who had caused the accident.

And in the mall, when Sharon had pulled Anna's seat away, Anna was the one who had turned it into a major scene. If she had just laughed at herself—or made a joke about Sharon "bumping" her chair—everything probably would have been fine. Sticky, but fine.

As for the soccer incident, Ms. Gilbert was right. It was just mud. *But I assumed everyone thought I was an idiot,* Anna realized. And she had continued to think it even after Carrie and Theresa had sat and worked with her in social studies and Matt Dana had kept her company on her way home.

None of them seemed to think any less of Anna because of all the things Sharon had said and done. *So why should I?* Anna asked herself. Zadie was right. The next time Sharon tried to make trouble for Anna, Anna wasn't going to let her. And that was that.

Anna looked down at her work sheet. *Write two sentences using compound verbs,* she read. She had started to write down the first sentence when she noticed a few people across the room giggling and staring at her. Then she saw Maria Mancini pass a folded-up piece of paper back to Lauren Graham.

Lauren unfolded the paper, read it, and smirked. Then she passed it back to Claudia Murray, who chuckled and continued it on to the next row.

Anna wasn't sure what was going on, but it obviously had something to do with her. Everybody who had read the note kept glancing in her direction and cracking up. She tried to concentrate on her work sheet, but she couldn't help feeling like everyone in the room was staring at her and laughing—probably because they were.

When the note finally made it to her side of the room, Anna couldn't wait to get her hands on it. She heard Matt Dana unfolding it behind her and waited. Any second now he would be passing it forward. Or so Anna thought.

Anna waited one minute. Then she waited two more. Finally, after five minutes had passed, she turned her head slightly and whispered, "Where is it?"

"What?" Matt asked.

"The note!" Anna hissed. "Where is it?"

"Anna," Mrs. Wessex called. "Please work on your own."

"Yes, Mrs. Wessex," Anna said. She picked up her pencil and tried to get back to work, but it was no use. On the corner of her paper, she wrote, *Give it to me!* Then she ripped it off and tossed it onto Matt's desk. For some reason, that made the whispers on the other side of the room grow louder.

"Okay, class, settle down," Mrs. Wessex said. "We only have a few minutes left."

Anna checked the clock. It was almost

lunchtime. Just then, a tiny slip of paper landed on her desk.

*You don't want to see it,* Matt had written. Anna flipped the scrap over. *YES, I DO!!!* she wrote in huge letters. Then she tossed the note back to Matt again. As she did, the bell rang to signal the end of class. Everyone was up immediately and rushing for the door.

"Ooh, Anna," Kimberly said as she walked by. "I had no idea."

"You might want to be a little more careful with your secret notes," Sharon added. Maria and Lauren giggled as they walked past, and a few other girls did, too.

"What are they talking about?" Anna demanded, turning to Matt.

"It's stupid," he said. "Just ignore them."

"Where's the note?" Anna growled.

"You really want to see it?" Matt asked.

"Yes!"

"All right," he said with a shrug, and he dropped it on her desk. "See you at lunch," he added on his way out the door.

Anna sat back down and unfolded the note so quickly, she almost tore it.

"Anna?" Mrs. Wessex said. "It's lunchtime. You should get to the cafeteria."

"I will," Anna assured her. "I just have to read something really quick." She looked down at the piece of paper in her hands and almost gasped. It said:

*Dear Matt,*
*I'm so glad I met you. You're the best skateboarder ever and the cutest guy in the whole school. I miss you when we're not together. Will you be my boyfriend?*
*Love,*
*Anna*

Zadie, who had been napping inside Anna's desk, stretched her arms above her head and yawned. "What's going on?" she asked. "Isn't it lunchtime yet?"

Anna didn't even bother to answer her. She just sat staring at the note with its loopy letters written in purple gel pen. *Sharon,* she thought. *How can she be so mean?*

"Hey—what's that?" Zadie asked. She jumped up onto the desk and then onto Anna's hand. "'Dear Matt,'" she started reading aloud. "Uh-oh. The Wicked Witch strikes again, huh?"

"Something like that," Anna muttered.

"So, what are you going to do about it?" Zadie asked.

"Die," Anna answered.

"What?!" Zadie screamed. "That's it? I thought we went over this yesterday! She can't make a fool out of you without your help! So what are you going to do? Help her? Or stop her?"

Anna looked at the note again. Everyone else seemed to think she had really written it. And if she didn't say anything, they were going to go right on thinking it—which was exactly what Sharon wanted. Well, for once, Sharon wasn't going to have things her way.

"I'm going to stop her," Anna said. And she stood up and headed for the cafeteria.

As she walked into the huge room, her knees felt just about ready to buckle. But Anna forced herself to keep going. Most of the fifth graders were already sitting down, so Anna walked straight through the lunch line and headed for where Sharon and her friends and Matt and his friends always sat.

"Excuse me," she said, standing at one end of the long table. Everyone kept talking. Anna cleared her throat. "Um, excuse me," she said again. A few people looked at her, but most of them were still gabbing.

She walked over to an empty seat next to Carrie. "Is anyone sitting here?" she asked.

"Actually, I was saving it for you," Carrie said.

"Good," Anna replied, but instead of sitting, she stood up on the chair so that she was towering above the rest of the table. Then she stuck her thumb and forefinger in her mouth and whistled the way her brother had taught her.

Like magic, everyone at the fifth-grade tables went silent. Anna swallowed hard. She wanted them to listen, but she hadn't realized just how weird it would feel to be addressing her whole class. Anna unfolded the note Sharon had written and cleared her throat.

"You can do it," Zadie whispered. "Here—take this." She placed a second piece of paper on top of the one Anna was holding. Then she jumped into Anna's jeans pocket and disappeared.

Anna looked at the paper Zadie had given her and smiled. *Perfect,* she thought. Then she cleared her throat again. "Um, for anyone who was just in Mrs. Wessex's room for English, I, um . . . wanted to talk about this." She held up the note that had been passed around the room.

A few people giggled, and Sharon smiled. "We've already seen it, Anna." She placed her hand over her heart dramatically. "Your feelings for Matt are no secret."

"Good," Anna said, eliciting a few more laughs. For a second she was worried that everyone was going to start talking again, but Theresa shushed everybody, and it was silent.

"Thanks," Anna whispered, glancing down at Theresa. Then she stood up straight. "What I mean is, I'm glad that most of you have seen it, because I just want to point a few things out."

Sharon squinted at her. It was a mini–death glare—a confused one—but Anna tried to ignore it.

"First of all," Anna said. "This is my notebook." She held up a dark blue binder and opened it. "As you can see, I use *white* lined paper. But this note is written on yellow."

"So?" Sharon said.

"Hold on—there's more," Anna said. "Second, it's written in purple gel pen, and I don't even have one of those." Some of the kids had started talking again, and Anna knew she had to get to the good stuff fast—before she lost them.

"Third, if you look at the handwriting in my notebook, you can see that I write really small. This note is written in big round letters."

"Maybe that's because you were so *in love* when you wrote it," Sharon suggested, drawing more giggles from the crowd.

"Actually, I thought maybe it was because *you* wrote it," Anna said. Immediately, the laughter stopped.

"You think *I* wrote it?" Sharon snapped.

"Well, you do use yellow notebook paper," Anna said. "Plus, you make big round letters, and you have a purple gel pen."

"No, I don't," Sharon sneered.

"Really?" Anna asked. "Then . . . how did you write this note to Kimberly?" She held up the paper Zadie had given her for everyone to see, then began passing it around. It was just a short one asking if Kimberly wanted to go to the mall after school, but the handwriting, the paper, and the pen all matched the note to Matt Dana perfectly.

"Where did you get that?" Sharon demanded.

Anna smirked. "Let's just say you should be more careful with your secret notes," she said. She stepped down and watched as the two notes Sharon had written made their way around the fifth-grade tables. Everyone was laughing—but for once, it wasn't at her.

Theresa and Carrie smiled over at her, and

they both gave her thumbs-up signals. Anna grinned and gave one back. "Go get your lunch," Carrie said. "We'll save your seat."

"Okay," Anna said, and she headed for the back of the line. "Hey, Zadie," she called, pretending to cough into her hand. "Did you hear that? I did it." Anna looked down at her pants pocket, half expecting the little angel to jump out with a tub of popcorn or some other kind of junk food clutched in her hand. But there was no sign of movement.

"Zadie?" she said again. Nothing.

Anna reached into her pocket carefully, but she didn't find Zadie. Instead she found one of the silver angel charms from her necklace. Anna felt the smooth metal between her thumb and forefinger, then flipped the charm over. On the back, the following words were engraved:

*Stand up, be strong,*
*and every once in a while,*
*eat dessert first!*

Anna clutched the charm in her hand and smiled. She was sad that Zadie was gone, but at the same time, she understood that she didn't need her anymore. She was going to be just fine on her own.

On her way through the lunch line, Anna grabbed an extra cookie—in honor of her tiny friend. When she got to the cashier, Matt Dana was in line behind her. He had come up for a second helping of apple crisp.

"Hey," he said, tapping Anna on the shoulder. "That took guts."

"Thanks," Anna replied.

"You'll be on the half-pipe in no time," he added with a grin.

Anna just laughed. But she thought, *Who knows? Maybe I will.* She walked back to the table where she'd just addressed the whole fifth grade and took her seat next to Carrie.

"That sounds fun," Theresa was saying to Sharon.

"Yeah, it should be cool," Sharon agreed. She glanced over at Anna with a bit of a scowl, but she didn't say anything.

"What should be cool?" Anna asked.

Sharon stared at her for a second, and Anna wasn't sure she was going to answer. "We're having a soccer game after school," she said finally. "Fifth graders against the sixth graders."

"You should play, Anna," Carrie said. She turned to Sharon. "Do we still need more people on our team?"

Sharon eyed Anna, then shrugged. "I guess," she said. "As long as you're not worried about getting dirty," she added.

"I can avoid the puddles if you can," Anna said, holding Sharon's gaze, and to her surprise, Sharon actually cracked a hint of a smile.

"No problem," she said. "Game's at three-thirty. Come on, Kimberly." Sharon and her number-one fan got up and headed back to the lunch line—probably to snag a Popsicle or something for dessert.

Anna unwrapped her first M&M cookie and took a bite. Sure, Sharon hadn't apologized to her—and Anna was pretty sure she never would—but somehow Anna felt like they had reached an agreement. It seemed obvious that they weren't going to be best friends or any-thing, but at the very least, it looked like they might be able to get along. And that was more than enough for Anna.

She took another bite of her cookie and thought about the charm in her pocket. Zadie was right. Eating dessert first was actually a pretty good idea.

# Get Ready for Charm Club
# Book #2:
# unicorn

"And in conclusion, with her great outfits and cool eyeliner, Cleopatra was a woman we can all admire." Sharon looked at the class and smiled proudly. "That's it—I'm done."

"Well, thank you, Sharon," Mrs. Wessex said as Sharon collected her notes and walked back to her seat. "That was certainly an interesting topic to choose for your Egyptian history presentation. Okay, class, who's next? Any volunteers?"

Carrie looked down at the poster on her desk and pretended to examine it. *Don't pick me. Don't pick me. Don't pick me.* Carrie knew if she made eye contact, all would be lost. But then she accidentally glanced up and . . .

"Carrie, that poster you've made looks beautiful, and I'm really looking forward to hearing your report on King Tut. Why don't you go next?"

"Um, okay." Carrie carried her poster and her note cards up to the front of the room. Her heart felt like it was going to pound itself right out of her chest. Her hands were shaking so hard, she had trouble balancing her poster against the blackboard. She faced the class and took a deep breath.

"Okay. So. Um. I'm doing my report on Ting Kut. . . ." Carrie could feel her face getting red. Was the room always this hot? She was starting to sweat. "I mean, uh . . . I'm doing my report on King Tut." Carrie looked down at the note card she was holding in front of her. Mrs. Wessex had said they shouldn't write out their whole report, just a few notes to help them remember what they wanted to say. "Memory joggers" was what Mrs. Wessex had called them. The night before, when Carrie was preparing for her presentation, she'd felt so confident, she hadn't bothered to write down many notes. But now, looking at her note card, which contained only a few random phrases and dates, she had no idea what she was going to say. "So, King Tut was this, um . . . king whose last name was, uh, Tut and . . ." She squinted at the note card. *Oh, no!* Why hadn't she written more neatly? She could barely even read her own handwriting. And what was that written there in the bottom corner? It looked like it said *ramen soup,* but that didn't even make any sense! Carrie rested her hands on the desk in front of her. She suddenly felt really dizzy.

"Carrie? Are you all right?" Mrs. Wessex asked, a concerned look on her face. "You're a bit flushed."

Carrie looked up at the class. Everyone was staring at her!

"Carrie?" Mrs. Wessex asked again. "Are you feeling okay?"

"Um—no," Carrie stammered. "You're right. I'm sick. I should probably go to the nurse. I should probably go right now." And with that, Carrie walked quickly toward the door, blood pounding in her ears. *Please, please, please do not let me trip on my way out.*

Anna raised her hand.

"Yes, Anna?"

"Mrs. Wessex, I can walk Carrie to the nurse if you want. She really doesn't look well."

"I suppose that would be all right," Mrs. Wessex said. "Please make sure she gets there safely. Feel better, Carrie. Do I have a volunteer to go next?"

As soon as they were out in the hallway, Carrie's pounding heart started quieting down. Anna turned to Carrie with a concerned look on her face.

"Hey, are you better?" Anna asked, putting her hand on Carrie's shoulder.

Carrie nodded silently. Now that she was out of the classroom, she felt kind of silly about how much she'd freaked out before.

"You're not *really* sick, are you?" Anna continued. "I thought maybe you didn't have a chance to finish planning your presentation last night or something."

"But that's just *it*," Carrie said miserably. "I *did* finish my presentation. I've been working on it for weeks, and I had it down perfectly last night. But when I got up there, I just froze. And now everyone's probably laughing at me!"

"Don't worry about it," Anna said. "At least you didn't fall over in front of the whole class or burp really loud or something! Besides, everyone is so worried about giving their own presentation, I doubt most people were even paying much attention."

Carrie nodded, even though she didn't quite

believe it. "You know what the dumbest part is? Now that I'm not in front of the class, I suddenly remember *everything* I was going to say. I bet I could do my whole report right here in the hallway without even looking at any stupid note card. But being up in front of everyone, I just completely froze!"

"Sounds like you just had a little case of stage fright. It's not a big deal. . . ."

"Easy for *you* to say."

A mysterious little smile suddenly came over Anna's face.

"Hey, hold up a second," she said. "When my friends found out I was moving away, they gave me this angel necklace. See?" Anna pulled the sparkling necklace out from the collar of her shirt.

"Um, sure. It's pretty," Carrie said, sounding confused.

"One of the charms, uh, fell off, and I attached it to this bracelet." Anna held out her wrist so Carrie could have a look. "Do you want to borrow it for a while? When I first moved here, I had a pretty rough time for a while. But it really, uh, helped me out. Maybe it will help you, too!" Carrie watched as Anna unhooked a pretty silver bracelet from around her wrist. It was a charm bracelet with a tiny angel charm dangling in the middle.

"Uh . . . okay. Thanks," Carrie said. She didn't want to make Anna feel bad—she was obviously trying to help. But Carrie really didn't see how a *bracelet* was going to help her with her stage fright. Not knowing what else to do, Carrie held out her arm, and Anna fastened the bracelet around her wrist. It glittered in the sunlight.

Anna and Carrie walked the rest of the way to the nurse's office. "Well, I guess I should go back to class now," Anna said. "Good luck." And then Anna winked at her and walked away.

"Bye," Carrie said out loud. Was she imagining things, or was Anna acting a little bit funny? *Unless this bracelet makes Mrs. Wessex stop assigning oral reports from now until the end of time, I'm not sure it will be much help.*

*WILL A LITTLE CHARM MAGIC BE ENOUGH TO HELP CARRIE WITH HER PROBLEM? FIND OUT IN CHARM CLUB BOOK 2: UNICORN*